BY THE SAME AUTHOR:

Mattimeo
Mossflower
Redwall

Seven Str
& Ghostly

Seven Strange & Ghostly Tales

Brian Jacques

Philomel Books
New York

First American Edition published in 1991 by Philomel
Books, a division of the Putnam & Grosset Group,
200 Madison Avenue, New York, NY 10016. Simultaneously
published in Great Britain by Hutchinson Children's Books,
London. Printed in the United States.

Library of Congress Cataloging-in-Publication Data
Jacques, Brian.
    Seven strange and ghostly tales / by Brian Jacques. p.   cm.
    Summary: A collection of seven creepy stories.
    ISBN 0-399-22103-4
    1. Ghost stories. English.   2. Children's stories, English.
    [1. Ghosts—Fiction.   2. Short stories.]   I. Title.
    PZ7.J15317Se   1991
    [Fic]—dc20   91-9889 CIP AC

10   9   8

Contents

1

This is a cautionary tale, young folk,
and must not be treated as a joke.
Let us then draw up a treaty
against all those who like graffiti.
Each pencil mark, each can of spray,
so difficult to wipe away;
each vandal going through "a phase"
that some poor cleaner must erase;
I beg you, shun the felt-tipped pen,
for when a wall's defaced, what then?
Do you seriously think society will say,
"How wonderful! How marvelous! Joey Rools Okay."
Why must the scribblers leave their marks for all to see,
thinking perhaps to gain themselves fame eternally?
Put aside that marker! Start a clean new slate—
and keep it clean, or you may share
the following scribbler's fate!

The Fate of Thomas P. Kanne

It was a quiet, grey Tuesday toward the end of the Christmas holidays. Turkeys had been devoured, gifts exchanged, and the festive season had tailed away into mundane January. Parents swept the last of the Christmas tree pine needles out of the carpet, while vowing to start dieting. As for the children, they were complaining that the batteries in their new toys had run out. Everybody was disgruntled, disillusioned and disappointed with the whole process of Yuletide. The fun, laughter and fairy lights would not return for nearly a whole long year.

None of this ever bothered Mr. Bausin, going about the same daily ritual he performed in his timeless world of Middlechester Museum: unlocking the great doors, checking the central heating gauges, switching the automatic alarm system back and forth to test it, and tidying the rows of brightly colored pamphlets and folders on the information desk. Christmases came and went; they were none of his business—the museum was his world. He lived in the apartment alone and self contained on the second floor, trusted completely by the administrators and curators. Mr. Bausin was totally devoted to his job as caretaker attendant of Middlechester Museum. His dark, muddy eyes smoldered with anger as he took solvent and a nylon pan-scrubber to the graffiti message sprayed on an Italian marble portal column.

PHANTOM SNAKE RULES!

He had missed that one. His anger was directed not at the writer, but at himself for the oversight. Mr. Bausin smiled a dark, secret smile as he scrubbed to erase the black auto enamel. Some sixth sense told him that soon, maybe even today, on this lackluster, humdrum Tuesday, he would finally meet his archenemy.

The Phantom Snake, always the same name. It had begun about two years back; the name began appearing all over his beloved museum. Sometimes in felt-tip, other times in thick blue luggage marker, more often than not in hard-to-remove air-drying car spray paint.

Phantom Snake!

Scrawled on glass exhibit cases, pamphlets and exit signs, written on marble statues, daubed on floors, walls, doors and stairways. One time it had actually been found in the left-hand corner of a priceless Renaissance screen. The head curator was furious. Experts were called in at great cost to remove the offending signature and restore the ancient work to its former beauty. Mr. Bausin had been reprimanded by the administration for letting such a thing happen. That day he had sworn on oath to his secret and dark gods: one day he would put an end to the Phantom Snake forever.

Yet the graffiti continued to appear, Bausin keeping one step ahead of the angry administration by erasing it quickly wherever he found it. And now with the museum's Egyptian Exhibition opening, Mr. Bausin feared greatly lest the holy relics of that high far-gone age would be a target for the depredations of the Phantom Snake. Not if he had anything to do with it! To be guardian over the priceless artifacts of Ancient Egypt was a sacred trust.

When he had removed the graffiti Mr. Bausin roamed through the Egyptian Exhibition, fondly checking each display: papyrus scrolls, reed model

3

boats, vases and urns, sacred scarabs and decorated amulets. Treading softly, he followed the wall of bas relief hieroglyphics around to the sarcophagus of the boy king Ahminrahken. Without the protection of a glass case the figure lay in solitary splendor, its open casket decorated in now faded colors. The whole tableau represented an inner sanctum of some pyramid tomb in the Valley of the Kings, with models of the old gods standing on the sandy floor, Set, Anubis, Horus and Osiris, guarding the resting place. Mr. Bausin took it all in slowly, finally easing silently out to resume his duties. And to watch and wait for the Phantom Snake.

Thomas P. Kanne noisily sucked the last of his milkshake through a straw as he sat watching the citizens of Middlechester going about their daily business. Through the plate-glass café window he could see policemen, housewives, bus drivers and road sweepers, a fair cross section of the community, carrying out their allotted chores. Blissfully unaware that they were being watched by the Phantom Snake.

He chuckled inwardly. Thomas P. Kanne, Phantom Snake. He was writing his own name rearranged into an anagram for them all to see, yet they could not solve it. Sheer brilliance on his part. He had known other graffiti writers, idiots, two of them from the same grade as he at school, who had gone about spraying their names all over town. It amazed him how they could reach the ripe old age of thirteen and still remain such fools. They had been caught easily, and now they were feeling the wrath of parents, teachers, social workers and even the police. But still nobody knew who the Phantom Snake was. None of them were clever enough to realize that it was an anagram of his own name.

4

Thomas secretly wrote the signature on the plastic counter in ballpoint before climbing down from the tall stool to venture out into the drab, chilly Tuesday afternoon. He wandered about the town center, marking each of his triumphs. His signature was on the bronze buttock of a water nymph in the district fountain. There was another one right across the center of a cough syrup advertisement, complete with a snaky mustache on the little girl whose mother was administering the soothing dose. Then there was the one that adorned the Town Hall steps, a letter upon each stair. They had removed it twice, but he had resprayed it each time. Nobody could catch the Phantom Snake. Thomas had thought of cryptically changing his logo to the drawing of a snake with the letter P at its head and an S at its tail. He rejected the idea — It would be lost on the stolid, unimaginative adults of Middlechester. Quietly, unobtrusively, he was sidling toward a large limousine parked outside the King's Head Hotel. It was white. Pure white!

Thomas looked like any enthusiastic schoolboy admiring a new Rolls Royce. He peered in the tinted windows at the walnut dashboard and morocco upholstery, before sidling round to the farside of the hood. Nobody was watching. He leaned over, as if inspecting the flying lady symbol on top of the radiator grille. Popping off the top of his broad red luggage marker, he executed a swift Phantom Snake signature on the gleaming white bodywork. The deed was done!

He slipped quickly away and sat on a bench outside the library, from where he could review the results of his handiwork. A man emerged from the hotel and, without noticing the signature, got straight into the Rolls and drove off. Thomas laughed inwardly. Short-sighted

5

idiot! He'd soon realize that the Phantom Snake had struck again.

The library bench was no fun, his signature had long ago been carved deeply into its woodwork with a sharp craft knife. Thomas strolled about feeling slightly ill at ease. It was getting all too easy, and he had covered the most prominent and important sites in town. Riding up the escalator in the shopping mall, he listened to the conversation of two women in front of him.

"Just look at this, Lil, 'Phantom Snake' done in white all the way round the banister rail. It's disgraceful, if you ask me."

"Right, you'd wonder what his parents are thinking about. I'd Phantom Snake him. I'd tan his hide if he were one of mine!"

"Me too. Mark it and destroy it, the young hooligan. It was never like that in our day. We were well behaved. Of course it was different then."

Thomas followed them, licking one of his ready-made stickers. As soon as the chance presented itself he bumped cleverly into the back of the one called Lil.

"Oops! Sorry. Excuse me."

They hustled awkwardly around each other, Lil smiling indulgently at the polite young man as he extricated himself and walked off. Lil and her friend carried on, still gossiping, unaware that one of them had a Phantom Snake sticker prominently displayed on her back.

Thomas turned to watch them, shaking his head knowingly. It was indeed all becoming too easy, the number of signatures dotted about the mall was clear evidence of this.

Thomas was halfway through completing a large and

elaborate signature on a *January Sale* sign posted on a boutique window, when the assistant's hand descended upon his shoulder.

"Gotcha, young fell—!"

Instinctively he relaxed and fell to the floor before the woman's hand could find a firm grip. Wriggling free, he scrambled away into the crowds of shoppers, the woman running behind him shouting, "You'll clean that off! Come back here!"

She was yelling and pointing at Thomas; a security man ran toward him from another direction; people were turning to stare at him. With his heart pounding wildly Thomas dashed onto an escalator—it was coming up, not going down! Disregarding the astonished folk on the moving staircase, he battled his way down, leaping clumsily against the rising stairs. The security man pulled out a two-way intercom; pushing buttons, he began speaking instructions to his colleagues.

Thomas made it to the ground-floor level, where he stumbled and fell. Adults stood open mouthed as he sprang to his feet, twisting and weaving among the bargain hunters through the brightly lit welter of arcades and shops. He took a right, then a quick left and another right turn, suddenly diving into a self-service cafeteria. Immediately slowing his breakneck pace he casually picked up a tray and joined the line of customers, regulating his breathing so that it sounded normal, though his chest still heaved and his hands trembled. Choosing a cream doughnut and a glass of orange juice, Thomas seated himself at a table with a family group. All the tables were fairly crowded, so he went unnoticed.

Licking cream from his fingers, Thomas watched the

7

security guard outside the window. He was joined by another one. They looked this way and that, conversed with each other, pressed more buttons on their intercoms, then went off in opposite directions.

The moment of danger had passed; Thomas relaxed. Finishing his orange juice he got up and carried two grocery bags for a young mother who was encumbered by an infant in a stroller. Together they walked out to the car park, and he helped her to fold up the stroller, stowing it with the groceries on the backseat of her car, a small hatchback. Thomas walked off in complete safety, her thank yous ringing in his ears. Nobody could catch the Phantom Snake!

A strange excitement began tingling through Thomas. Instead of discouraging him, his narrow escape had had the opposite effect. He felt reckless and daring, ready for more adventure. But where, and how? A nearby billboard with posters of local events provided the answer.

MIDDLECHESTER MUSEUM
EGYPTIAN EXHIBITION.
9:30 A.M. to 5:00 P.M.
Mon to Fri throughout January. Admission free.

Of course! Thomas hurried to meet the new challenge. Many times he had dashed off his logo only seconds ahead of his favorite adversary, the watchful old attendant.

From the edge of the lawn in front of the museum Thomas watched a group being shepherded inside by the grey-haired, swarthy complexioned Bausin. Then he began his own preparations. Like a bullfighter before the corrida Thomas went through the ritual of readying

8

himself. Giving his spray can a good shake he stowed it in the inside pocket of his baggy zip jacket. Next he undid the red and blue luggage markers. Working swiftly, he rolled back his jacket sleeves, wedging each marker up into the elasticized wristbands, taking care to roll the sleeves slightly downwards to disguise them. Two felt-tip pens, one green, the other black, went with the ballpoint into his back jeans pockets, together with his signed adhesive stickers. Thomas P. Kanne was ready. Things were certainly heating up for a dull post-Christmas Tuesday!

Mr. Bausin noticed the youth who tacked on to the back of the group he was conducting into the Egyptian Exhibition. Their eyes met briefly; each looked away with a secret smile. The attendant coughed importantly and began his commentary, "Many reliable experts say that life began in the East, and certainly there is ample documented evidence that for thousands of years before the birth of Christ, a large civilization flourished in Egypt, land of the Kings. . . ."

The voice droned on as people consulted their pamphlets at the appropriate points. Thomas sized up the passage leading to the burial chamber, his fertile mind racing ahead. There was an unprotected terra-cotta vase—the black felt-tip would do for that. And what about a sticker for the center of the glass case top, where it would be flanked by four sacred scarabs? Thomas stood at the back of the group, close to the raised images on a wall of reproduction figures, fashioned in resin, forming the entrance to the burial chamber. He worked swiftly with the black felt-tip as the attendant's drone washed over the attentive party. "Ra, giver of life, the Sun God; Horus the hawk-headed figure; Set the cat, a popular creature in Egyptian religion and mythology—all of these had their parts to play in the temples of Karnak. However, to my mind the most potent of the Egyptian deities is Anubis, the jackal-headed man. . . ."

The Phantom Snake had already struck!

The signature had been swiftly scrawled along the back of a snake featured on the resin wall. Thomas looked up to see Mr. Bausin looking directly at him, and stared insolently back. The attendant could not possibly have seen him writing, shielded as he was by the backs of an elderly couple. The party moved on.

Thomas felt slightly mystified; Bausin had looked right at him. That one look had said it all: he knew Thomas was the Phantom Snake. Yet it was not uneasiness that possessed Thomas, it was defiance, a feeling that his skills as a secret graffiti artist had been noted, but not acknowledged. This was altogether different from some boutique lady who had nearly got lucky in the mall. This was a real contest of wit and cunning.

Thomas decided to keep his opponent on tenterhooks. He stayed with the group, noting opportunities, though not doing anything as of yet. He felt increasingly irritated that the attendant sensed this and had begun ignoring him.

The Phantom Snake was not to be disregarded!

Casually Thomas detached himself from the group and strolled back into the main museum. He was determined that his enemy would long remember a dull Tuesday in January when his sanctum had been invaded by an expert. Thomas sprayed part of the rib bone of a dinosaur black, leaving his signature in red marker upon the air-drying enamel where it could not be missed. Taking the stairs two at a time, he bounded

10

to the upper floor. He signed again, this time on the ecru satin seat of a hansom cab. The front of a glass case of butterflies caught his creative imagination, and he took his time with this one, carefully signing so that it looked like small moths in alternate red and blue luggage marker with touches of the black and green felt pens here and there. Pretty! He stood back critically and cast an eye over his handiwork.

Down below in the Egyptian Exhibition Mr. Bausin was completing his tour of the artifacts, speeding up his narrative now that he realized the boy had left the group. Bausin was certain that Thomas had not left the museum; his inner senses told him so. Keeping remarkably calm, the attendant paid strict attention to his duties and his public. He completed the commentary and walked with the party to the main door. Refusing a tip from a young couple, he saluted lightly as they left the building, repeating his usual remarks automatically with a friendly smile, "Thank you, call again. Thank you, goodbye!"

When the last one had gone, the smile was replaced by a look as cold and grim as a damp mortuary slab. Mr. Bausin closed the high double doors. They shut with an echoing boom in the stillness of the museum. He turned the key in the lock and slid the well-oiled steel bolts into place. Striding purposefully toward the stairway, his heels clicked ominously against the polished granite floor.

Thomas P. Kanne had been enjoying himself upstairs. He was putting the finishing touches to a masterpiece in black, blue and red upon a Moorish shield of Toledo steel when he heard the dull boom of the main doors shutting. He cut across the passage and through

11

another room to the window, just in time to see the visitors disperse and walk off into the darkening early evening. Thomas felt a delicious charge of danger and imminent peril course along his spine. His sneakers made virtually no sound as he hurried to the second-floor stairwell, listening to the click of advancing heels. Poking his head around the corner of the stairs, he watched the attendant mounting the bottom steps. Impudently he scribbled broadly over the floor of the stairwell.

PHANTOM SNAKE RULES FOREVER!

Darting into a roomful of exhibits, he lay flat beneath a Chippendale chaise longue, making himself small on the polished wooden floorboards as he peered at the doorway.

Mr. Bausin entered the room slowly. He looked carefully around, noticing each signature, each desecration of his sacred museum and its precious specimens. Standing in the doorway he called out in a singsong voice, as if addressing a naughty child, "Come on out, I know you're in here."

Thomas lay still, knowing the attendant had not seen him. He was looking at the back of Bausin's shoes—the attendant had not turned around yet, so how could he have spotted him; it was all a bluff. Mr. Bausin strode further into the room, first going to the left, then to the right. Finally he walked across to the window and stood looking out, just as Thomas had done. Outside the gloomy twilight seeped into January darkness.

Thomas rolled from under the chaise longue like a cat. Silently he rose to his feet. Creeping stealthily from the room, he glanced over his shoulder to see the

12

attendant caretaker, still standing with his back to him, facing the window. Thomas made a waving snake motion with one arm at his adversary's back before going downstairs.

Mr. Bausin smiled with his lips, his eyes remained as citrines as he watched the reflection of the boy in the darkened windowpane. Walking unhurriedly to the entrance, he switched off the lights and locked the door from the bunch of keys he carried on his belt.

Thomas had gone back downstairs. Bounding silently along, he ran to the entrance doors and tried the handles just to make sure they were locked. The back of his knees quivered as he heard his pursuer descending the stairs with heel-clicking precision. Thomas dodged behind one of the fluted inner entrance columns—it was too slim to provide total concealment, but it was the only immediate cover. Now Bausin was nearly downstairs. Thomas held his breath, hoping that he would not be seen. Panic was about to rise gurgling in his throat when the footsteps stopped. He breathed a sigh, half of relief, half of disgust with himself for being so frightened. Squinting around the column he watched Bausin remount the stairs and enter a side room on the mezzanine floor.

The saturnine caretaker inspected the room, which contained prehistoric fossils arranged in wall cases. The central piece of the display was a replica pterodactyl, suspended from the ceiling on thin wires. Satisfied that there was no secret hiding place within the open square of the displays, Bausin left, taking care to lock the door behind him. Leaving thus another place the Phantom Snake could not wriggle into.

Thomas had taken advantage of his pursuer's detour. Deserting the scant safety of the inner columns he glanced swiftly left and right, trying hard to outwit his opponent. Keeping to the left of the main hallway he hurried past the Wonders of Steam room. Behind him he could hear the attendant descending the final stairs. Thomas dropped quickly behind a life-size bronze statue of Queen Victoria, knowing that if Bausin looked left from the foot of the stairs he would immediately see anyone out in the hall. Thomas could have cheered aloud when he heard the footsteps of the hunter go off down the right part of the hallway instead of the left. What chance did an attendant have against him, the Phantom Snake, who could slip out of any trap? He would find an open window, a fire escape, an unlocked exit and escape. He relaxed a little, looking up to find himself staring into Queen Victoria's left nostril; she was definitely not amused! Neither was Thomas P. Kanne a moment later when, with a click of the main switch, the lights went out, plunging the whole of Middlechester Museum into eerie darkness.

Mr. Bausin switched on his flashlight, and turning his key in the lock of the mid hall fire doors he isolated the entire right half of the museum. The field was rapidly narrowing. By the light of his flashlight he fastened the guard chain across the bottom of the stairs. It would not stop his quarry, but it might trip him in the darkness without a light to see where it was. Humming an old Egyptian folk tune to himself he set off to the left, sorting out the key to the Wonders of Steam room as he went. One more place to check; one more door to lock; one room less to hide in.

As he progressed down the hallway Thomas noticed that the walls were too smooth and the windows too high to reach. Judging by the scant light that filtered through their dusty panes they had probably been

14

locked for years too. Ignoring the Egyptian Exhibition he entered the room directly opposite. Thomas's nerve nearly deserted him when he bumped into a huge figure —in the dim light a King's Hussar with drawn sabre glared at him over a waxed handlebar mustache.

It took Thomas a moment or two to regain his composure, then he snorted silently. Imagine being scared of a dummy dressed in the relics of yesteryear – this was no way for the famous Phantom Snake to behave. He was halfway to opening a luggage marker when a movement on the opposite side of the room disturbed him. Somebody was actually there watching him. Thomas's hands began to tremble uncontrollably; the marker fell from his nerveless fingers. Slowly he summed up his last ounce of courage and turned to face the spectral figure in the darkened room.

It was a mirror!

A silly, stupid, foolish, long regimental mirror from some defunct officers' mess. He had been terrorized by his own reflection. Utterly disgusted with himself, he bent to retrieve the fallen luggage marker. Then the sounds began. Without warning an eerie chant boomed through the silence.

It rose and fell in an echoing muttered cadence, filling the museum hallway. With a panicked sob Thomas pelted off down the hall, his sneakers slapping hard against the floor.

Bausin lay in a prostrate position, his arms extended, palms open, as he chanted the last stanza of the secret rites to the old gods and the mummified boy Pharaoh. His voice rose and fell as he vowed retribution on the desecrater of the treasures from Karnak, pleading with the dark and forgotten deities to aid him. Satisfied he had done his duty, he picked up the flashlight and

15

resumed his tour. Searching the regimental room thoroughly he assured himself that his intended victim was not there. As he swung the door shut his foot came in contact with something . . . the red plastic top of a luggage marker. He pocketed it and locked the door.

Bausin continued down the hallway, leaving the rooms of the Egyptian Exhibition wide open. Unhurriedly he reached the end of the hall; there was only one way to go now. Down. Directing the flashlight on the black marble banister curving down into the museum basement he guided himself slowly downstairs, listening to the sounds of his prey, Thomas, scurrying about somewhere within the bowels of the building. Turning, he secured the guard chain across the top steps before continuing downward. The round golden orb of flashlight bobbed and danced around the stairwell, like a tiny offspring of Ra the Sun God guiding him.

Though it was unusual to perspire on a cold January night Thomas felt sweat running from his brow; he felt the beads drip onto his lips and licked them nervously. The rooms he looked in were all too small and bare to hide in, except for the one on the second right. There was an oil-fired central heating boiler which gave off a soft thrumming noise and a faint red glow; a table with a chair by it stood in a corner. Hearing the regular click of heels coming down the passage Thomas had no choice. He ducked under the table, crouching like a cornered animal. Bausin came onward, slow and relentless, checking each room thoroughly before locking it. First right, then first left, now second right. As he entered the room he was conscious of his quarry's presence.

Deliberately Bausin strode to the boiler, tapping the

gauges as if to check them, but listening keenly to the sound of Thomas dodging out of the room behind his back. The caretaker searched and locked each room until the whole basement was secured. He nodded in satisfaction at the sound of Thomas tripping over the guard chain on the top stair. Now the trap was complete. The Phantom Snake had only one last place to slither into.

Thomas entered the Egyptian Exhibition with two thoughts uppermost in mind. One, to give Bausin the slip; two, to find a phone somewhere so that he could call the police. A good story would be simple enough to invent: wandering about, forgot the time, locked in by mistake, very sorry to have caused any inconvenience. He peered into the darkness, trying to discern the shadowy shapes of the life-size objects. That one must be Horus, the hawk-headed god, he had read that on the plaque earlier today.

Click, click, click, click.

Bausin's slow, measured pace drew nearer, Thomas squeezed in beneath the scarab case. The clicking stopped and Thomas held his breath. Suppose he was locking the door. . . no he wasn't. The old fool, what was he up to now?

Complete silence. What if he'd tiptoed away, leaving Thomas to stew in his own fear. No, an old buffoon like him wouldn't have the subtle imagination. Maybe he was trying to outwit the Phantom Snake, or outwait him, one or the other. Seconds crept by like minutes, the minutes seemed to stretch into hours. Once or twice Thomas was forced to move from his cramped position, but still there was no sound.

Thomas P. Kanne reached a desperate decision; he would dash out! If the attendant was not there, so much

17

the better; he could search for a telephone. However, if he was still there waiting, Thomas would barge into him, trip him, grab the keys, knock him over, jump over him and dash off; there were many possibilities. Crawling from under the scarab case Thomas stretched himself to restore the circulation in his limbs. Putting his best foot forward into the darkness he muttered tightly through his teeth, "Ready, steady . . . Go!"

With all the speed he could muster Thomas dashed for the doorway. He could not stop as the shadowy bulk leapt out in front of him. His fearful wail mingled with the single, chilling growl the creature gave. The huge body pressing close to Thomas smelt fetid and musky. He felt his body crushed close up to it, steel fingers had him helpless in their vicelike grip. The sweat on Thomas's face turned to ice when he glimpsed the features of his captor. It was not human, it had the head of a great slavering dog! The jackal-like eyes burned hungrily; the big yellow fangs dripped saliva as its fearsome mouth panted hot breath into his nostrils; the black-tipped muzzle poked wetly against his cheek. Thomas fainted limply.

A voice was murmuring close by as Thomas's brain swam through a red mist of pain into consciousness.

"*O great Pharaoh, accept as a slave and a servant in the underworld this one who has desecrated thy shrine. He will serve thy every need and do thy bidding, for was it not his race who removed thee from Karnak, Valley of the Kings, resting place of thy mighty ancestors. O my master, it was I, Anubis, who ever watched over thee.*"

Thomas P. Kanne could not budge a single inch, he could not blink his eyes, even though they were open wide. His arms, legs and body were wound tightly with bandages from neck to toe; a gag had been forced into

18

his mouth. Bausin chanted as he laid out needles and vials of ancient embalming fluids. A single tear managed to well from the corner of his victim's eye as he listened to the jackal-headed man.

"O Ruler of Egypt, now thy slave will join thee in the underworld. I fill his veins with the mystic fluids which were administered to thee in death long centuries back. Accept my offering and be at peace in the houses of the dead, ere Ra the Sun God races across the skies in his fiery chariot."

Fright and fearsome terror gripped Thomas P. Kanne, together with an unbearable longing for his last day in this world as a human boy, even though it was only a dull Tuesday after the Christmas festivities. He felt the needle prick the side of his neck, then his whole body went as cold as ice. The gag was removed from his now speechless mouth and something metallic placed upon his tongue.

"Take this coin to pay the ferryman of the dark river for thy master's crossing into the underworld."

Thomas's head lolled from side to side as Anubis wrapped the smooth linen bandages in an upward swathe, carefully working his way from the neck up to the crown of the head.

Releasing a hidden catch, Anubis separated the sarcophagus of the boy Pharaoh into two halves. He lifted the mummified form of Thomas P. Kanne into the lower half of the deep coffin, then slid the top half back into place. The catch clicked shut, hiding all trace of the graffiti writer from the world forever.

A suggestion that the boy Pharaoh's mummy be protected by a glass case was accepted by the museum administrators. The possibility of it being vandalized was unthinkable. However, graffiti seemed to have died down of late, particularly the writings of the one called

19

Phantom Snake. It was at dead of night when the final graffiti message was written. It was carved underneath the base of the statue of Anubis, so it would not have been noticed by either the museum staff or the public. Mr. Bausin had taken loving care in scribing the message.

PHANTOM SNAKE RULES NO MORE.
BAUSIN IS ANUBIS!

2

My first is in victory, though not in battle.
My second's top mark, the start of an apple.
My third is in empty, and also in mitts.
My fourth is in pieces, but not in bits.
My fifth's in a needle, but not in its spelling.
My sixth's last in the water, first in repelling.
My seventh and last is a compass point
(Also found twice in "every joint").
So put me together, and I hear you say,
"You'll never see him around during the day."

What am I?

Jamie and the Vampires

"Jaymeeeee!"

Jamie was halfway across the lawn, ready to vault over the hedge, when his mother's call halted him. He raised his eyes to heaven.

"Jamie! Don't you dare jump over that hedge. Come back here this minute. Keep out of the flower bed. What did your father tell you only last night? 'Keep out of the flower bed,' he said. Why you can't walk down the path like any other perfectly normal human being I'll never know. . . ."

Jamie stood still resignedly, wondering why his mother had a voice like a rusty bathroom tap that never stopped leaking. "You're not listening to a word I'm saying, are you, my lad?" she continued. "Now come back here this instant and put this clean shirt on. The good Lord only knows what the neighbors must think of me, letting you run wild dressed like a tramp. That shirt needs a good wash." He winced as his mother grabbed him, pulling him into the house as she carried on nagging him. Her voice had changed from a rusty tap to a scrap metal breaking machine that still had two million tons of iron to pulverize.

"Just look at the color of your neck! It's a good job I caught you sneaking off, young man. That neck hasn't seen soap, water, or wash cloth today—I've never seen a tidemark like it in all my life. And have you taken your pills? No, you haven't taken them. Those teeth could do with a clean. What do you do with all that toothpaste? Eat it? You certainly don't clean your teeth with it, that's for sure. Remember what Doctor Hanley said, if you don't take your pills the allergy will start up again and you'll be sneezing all over me and your father.

22

When that starts you'll go straight up to bed and stay there. Wipe your feet before you come in here; I'm not slaving away cleaning the carpets just to have your muddy footprints all over my house. You'd be better off in a zoo. . . ."

In the space of the next ten minutes Jamie had his entire face, neck, cheeks and ears scrubbed, then his hands. His shirt was pulled from him and a clean one replaced it. A fresh handkerchief was stuffed in his pocket, pills and a drink of water forced down his protesting mouth; his teeth were rebrushed, clean socks thrust upon his feet and his shoes sprayed with Scuffguard. He fought his way to the door as his hair was brushed until tears sprang to his eyes and his scalp smarted. His mother restrained him while she did something unmentionable with a twisted apron corner to his left nostril, admonishing him endlessly as she applied the torture vigorously.

"Now you've got a clean handkerchief in your pocket, for goodness sakes use it! And another thing, don't let me hear of you hanging around with that gang from the arcade. Try and keep yourself clean for at least five minutes, and don't be late for lunch. Are you listening to me? Don't kick the toes out of those shoes, Heaven only knows where the next pair are coming from with the price of them these days. What about your homework? I'll bet you haven't even started it. Just because it's the beginning of the holidays don't think you can dodge homework. You mark my words, or you'll end up like that Monaghan, thick as two short planks and hanging about on street corners. . . ."

His mother retwirled her apron corner, and Jamie had visions of her stuffing it down his ear and pulling it out via the other one, in a sort of joint ear/

brain-cleaning operation. With a desperate twist he squirmed free of the maternal hands, bounding across the lawn to clear the garden hedge with a single flying leap. He jogged off down the road with his mother's voice following him on the summer breeze, a full octave higher and sounding this time like a runaway chainsaw.

"Wait till your father gets home, my lad! Blatant disobedience, that's what it is. You'll break your neck jumping over that hedge one of these days, then you'll have learned your lesson too late. Anyhow, you can stay home tomorrow and do your homework, I'll see to that. You can count on it, young man. . . ."

Jamie slowed to a walk as he neared the cemetery. Ruffling his hair wildly he jumped up and down in the dust, until the still wet Scuffguard had attained a reasonable coating of dirt. He threw back his head and yelled at the sun, "Yaaaah, mothers!"

Who needed them? He fondly imagined a motherless existence as he climbed over the high cemetery gates. Beds were more fun if they were unmade—you could keep lots of things in the folds of a quilt, soldiers, tanks and all that, like an army camp in the mountains. Without a mother his dad could go off to work every morning and he would get himself up out of bed. What was the problem? A can of cola from the fridge and some crackers, you didn't have to cook those. What about baked beans? He liked eating cold baked beans straight from the can with a spoon—they were good for you. He could wear black clothes, special ones that never needed washing, quit school, go to fast-food places if he needed a cooked meal, play his tapes aloud without the headphones, watch loads of TV, get clean when he went swimming at the gym—

"Jamie, over here!"

He banished the problem of mothers from his mind and ran leaping between headstones and crosses to the clump of rhododendrons at the back of the chapel. Monaghan and the rest of the gang were waiting for him. Jamie slumped down with his back against the chapel wall, hidden by the rhododendrons. It was the ideal meeting place for the gang. He could tell by their faces that something was going on.

"So, what's new?"

Kelly Ann giggled. "Shall we tell him?"

Jamie was irritated by her; she'd probably grow up to be just like his mother, he could tell. There was an expectant silence. Monaghan scraped moss from the chapel wall with his fingernail, his tone deceptively matter of fact as he announced, "We've found a vampire's tomb."

Jamie shielded his eyes from the sun as he looked up at the gang leader. "You've what?"

Kelly Ann wagged her head knowingly.

"We found a vampire's tomb. You never, cause you weren't here."

Jamie ignored her. He did not want to start an argument with Kelly Ann, she always got the better of him with her fund of smart remarks. He spoke directly to Monaghan.

"Is that right?"

"Yep."

"A real vampire's tomb!"

"Right."

Jamie shook his head in disbelief. He smiled through his tousled bangs. "Ah, you're kiddin' me."

Little Cliffie wet his finger and drew several swift crosses over his stomach. "We're not kiddin', cross my heart and hope t'die."

25

Jamie narrowed his eyes. "Well, where *is* this vampire's tomb?"

Kelly Ann pointed dramatically off to where the broken cemetery wall was met by the overgrowing woods.

"It's right over there in the bushes where no one ever goes."

Monaghan took out a broken penknife and began scraping his initials into the church wall. "Want me to show you it?"

Jamie stood up. "Come on then, I'm not scared."

As they walked across the graveyard, Paula and Gary, the remaining gang members, explained to Jamie, "We came through the woods this morning and climbed over the far side of the cemetery."

"Yeah, you should see the graves there, all foreign. Hungarian, I think. Vampires come from Hungaria, don't they?"

Kelly Ann scoffed. "It's not Hungaria, silly, it's Hungary."

Jamie paused by a marble angel with outspread wings.

"How d'you know it's Hungary if they're all foreign graves, Smartypants?"

"It said Magyar on some of them. Magyar's in Hungary, my big brother's stamp album says so. Smartypants yourself!"

Just like his mother, Kelly Ann had an argument and an answer for everything. Jamie walked the rest of the way in silence.

Monaghan pointed with the broken blade of his penknife at a rickety wood cross on an overgrown grave plot. "There's one of 'em, look. Zillibor Zorbigowitch or someone. See the funny writing? He died in 1902.

There's another one, that grey stone cross, two of 'em in there, they died in 1895 and 1898."

Jamie blew hair out of his eyes as he inspected the stone.

"Doesn't make 'em vampires though, does it? Just 'cause they're from Hungaria and died a long time ago."

Kelly Ann parted the edge of a vastly overgrown lilac bush.

"Well take a look at this one, Mr. Knowitall!"

It was not a grave, it was a tomb. Dark, mossy stonework, entwined with weeds and creepers. Two broad steps led up to a bronze door that had long ago acquired a patina of green verdigris. Jamie stood goggle eyed at the sight of the sinister stone heap. It resembled a small temple, squared off ledges and columns with kneeling angels at each corner. Even in the midday summer sun it was a fearsome vision. Monaghan tapped his broken blade against the bronze door.

"What d'you suppose this is?"

Jamie peered at the representation of a bird embossed upon the metal.

"It's an eagle, isn't it?"

Kelly Ann curled her lip and folded her arms.

"Shows how much you know. Huh, even little Cliffie knows what that is. Tell him, Cliffie, go on."

"It's a bat, a vampire's bat!"

Jamie borrowed Monaghan's knife and scraped at the bronze. He turned and shrugged, trying to redeem himself in the gang's eyes.

"Hard to tell, it's so old. Could be a bat, I suppose."

Monaghan folded his knife away.

"It's a vampire bat all right, I've seen them in books. Look at the bottom here, it says 'Magyar' in big letters and there's a sort of a round shape. Looks like a full moon if you ask me."

Jamie nodded his agreement. It was always best to nod when Monaghan said anything—he was the biggest and toughest of the gang.

"Oh yeah, right. Can you make out the names of the dead people?"

"Nope, all this green stuff's grown too thick around the letters. Bet they're Hungarians though, and look what Paula found on the steps."

Paula pulled a face, wringing her hands nervously.

"Yukk! I'm not touching that thing!"

Gary turned it over in the long grass with his foot. "Here it is."

It was a dead bat, a tiny pipistrelle. Jamie could not resist a smile as he watched them goggling at the pitiful carcass.

"Haha, bit little for a vampire bat, isn't it?"

Kelly Ann sniffed.

"You were a bit little for a boy when you were born, pity your brain never grew up."

Monaghan and the rest broke into raucous laughter. Immediately Jamie was put on the defensive; his cheeks flushed red.

"At least I'm not scared like you lot. I'm not frightened of a little dead bat on some moldy old foreign grave!"

"Yes you are!"

"No I'm not!"

"Are!"

"Not!"

Monaghan intervened. "Okay, let's see you sit alone on those steps for ten minutes if you're not scared."

Jamie plonked his behind firmly on the top step and

rammed his back hard against the bronze door.

"There. See!"

Monaghan stuffed his hands deep in his pocket and leaned forward, staring hard at Jamie.

"Right! You've got to stay there for ten full minutes all on your own. We'll walk to the arcade and back; that should take about ten minutes more or less."

"But I haven't got a watch. How'll I know when the ten minutes is up?"

Kelly Ann provided a solution. Jamie had known she would somehow.

"Sixty seconds in a minute, so if you count up to six hundred that should be ten minutes exactly. You can count, can't you?"

Jamie thrust his chin forward aggressively. " 'Course I can!"

"Well see you do!" She had got the last word in again; he wondered if she were a distant relation of his mother's.

After they had gone Jamie sat alone with his thoughts on the step of the tomb. The metal door felt like ice on his back . . . supposing it swung inward all of a sudden. He had seen that happen in a film on television. Moving forward, he sat on the bottom step, muttering quietly.

"Bet I've got that green stuff all over the back of my shirt, that'll give Mum something to shout about. Huh, I've missed lunch too, and my second lot of allergy tablets. She'll prob'ly hit the roof when I get home. What was that sound?"

A low moan issued from the nearby bushes.

Despite the warmth of the day Jamie felt ice-cold sweat prickling his forehead. He was about to galvanize his legs into action for a quick dash away from the tomb when he heard a stifled giggle from the thicket. His quick glance caught a flash of pink T-shirt.

Kelly Ann!

Straight away he relaxed. The gang was playing some sort of trick, trying to scare him off. But he resolved to sit tight.

The tiny dead bat was tossed out of the leafy screen. It landed floppily by his feet.

Jamie would show them. Smiling inwardly, he gave a massive yawn and snuggled down on the steps, pretending to be asleep.

"Jaaaaayyyymmmmeeeeewoooooooh!"

That was Monaghan's voice, he could tell it anywhere. Lying quite still, Jamie listened to the whispered conversation coming from the thicket.

"He's pretending to be asleep, the fool." (That was Kelly Ann.)

"Are you sure? He looks awfully still." (Little Cliffie.)

"Here, this'll move him!" (Monaghan.)

Jamie willed himself to remain still, even when the pebble thrown by Monaghan struck him on the arm.

"See, I told you there's something wrong, he's too still." (Cliffie.)

"Oh, don't be stupid. Can't you see he's playacting?" (Kelly Ann, who else.)

"Cliffie's right, we shouldn't have left him on his own. He *is* lying too still, I don't like it." (Good old Gary.)

Jamie heard them creeping out of their hiding place. They came toward where he was lying.

"Bet you when we turn him over there'll be two marks on his neck, an' blood too." Little Cliffie sounded really concerned.

They moved forward, rather subdued and scared. Jamie, timing the moment exactly right, leaped up with a scream. "Eeeeeeaaaaarrrrgggghhhhh!"

They panicked instantly, bumping into each other and crashing off into the bushes, even Kelly Ann. Jamie sat down straight-faced. "Five hundred and ninety-eight, five hundred and ninety-nine, six hundred! Well, here I am, gang, don't be afraid."

Little Cliffie, Paula and Gary grinned sheepishly. But Kelly Ann and Monaghan were seething. Jamie laughed aloud, pointing scornfully at them as he leaned against the bronze door of the tomb.

"Hahahaha! You should've seen your faces! What a load of old women, what a bunch of ninnies! Hahahaha!"

Little Cliffie laughed with him out of pure relief. "Er, haha, you mean you weren't scared?"

Jamie flipped the dead bat over with his toe. It went sailing through the air into the bushes.

"Me scared? You must be joking. What's to be scared of? A heap of stone with daft writing on it. Ha! No chance."

Monaghan shrugged. "Bet you'd be scared if it was dark."

Jamie missed the wink that passed between Monaghan and Kelly Ann. Bursting with confidence, he fell straight into their trap.

"Dark doesn't scare me. I'd come here any time!"

Kelly Ann was quick as a cat upon a rat. "Bet you wouldn't come here at midnight."

"Huh, ten, eleven, midnight, it doesn't bother me," Jamie replied airily.

Monaghan sneered trimphantly. "Okay, I'll bet you, in fact I'll *dare* you to come here at midnight when the church bell rings."

Jamie could see by Kelly Ann's and Monaghan's faces that he had fallen headlong into their snare. He could hardly believe his own ears as he heard himself answering in a still very cocky voice.

"All right, it's a bet!"

Mentally kicking his own backside he placed his hand over theirs on the cold stone vault and recited the gang's solemn oath with them.

"Take this bet, take this dare.
If you bet me I'll be there.
If I don't then you'll know why,
Cross my heart and hope to die."

Fingers were wetted and drawn across throats and over hearts. No more was said; they went their ways in silence.

Jamie wandered home with a sick feeling in the pit of his stomach. What a fool he had been, letting himself get tricked like that. There was no way anyone could back out on the dreaded double, a bet and a dare. Monaghan and Kelly Ann had fixed up the details; they were to wait for him by the cemetery gates; they had sworn a serious oath not to follow him into the cemetery. Jamie was to sit on the steps of the tomb for ten minutes as the clock struck twelve. At least he had the consolation of knowing there would be no stupid tricks to scare him. But midnight! He would have to find some way of sneaking out of the house, his mother and father would never allow him to roam loose at that hour. It was all right for the likes of Monaghan and Kelly Ann, they could hang around the streets or go anywhere they pleased without their parents giving a hoot. Maybe his mother had been right about hanging around with the arcade gang.

32

Jamie did not bother jumping the hedge or crossing the lawn. He slouched up the path to where his mother was waiting, lips tight, arms akimbo, ready to launch into her tirade.

"Do you know what time it is? Lunch went cold half an hour ago. Beautiful homemade chicken soup, all greasy and cold now. Just look at those shoes, you'd think they'd never been cleaned since I bought them. And what have you done to your hair? It looks as if a bird's been nesting in there. Five minutes later, my lad, and I'd have been along to that arcade place with a glass of water and these allergy tablets, make no mistake about that! You dirty little beast, what's all that green muck on the back of your clean shirt? I slave my fingers to the bone, washing, ironing, trying to keep you decent. Look at you! You're a disgrace to the family. . . ."

Jamie climbed the stairs to his room, his mother following behind, wagging her finger and carrying on like a pack of wolves chasing a sausage manufacturer.

"All right, that's it! You can stay in your room now for the rest of the day. I'll show you. And don't think you're getting away without eating my lovely chicken soup. I'll warm it up again. Now you can clean your room out; it's like a battlefield. Then you can get down to doing some homework. And don't entertain any ideas of slipping away to gallivant with that arcade lot, my lad. You can stay in all this evening too. If I told your father about the way you behave, he'd certainly have a word or two to say to you, he certainly would. . . ."

Jamie closed his bedroom door as the talking machine retreated downstairs, still carrying on like a

33

hi-fi with a busted needle. "I know lots of children who'd be very glad of a clean, decent home and loving parents to care for them. The trouble with you, young man, is that you've had it too easy, ten times too easy, a lot easier than I ever had it when I was your age, a lot easier, believe me. . . ."

Jamie lay back on his bed and tried to imagine his mother at the same age as himself. He found it practically impossible, though he bet himself that even as a baby she went about with a dustpan and broom in her hands, yes, and a bottle of allergy pills, looking for normal children to dose against allergies, and grabbing children from baby carriages, twisting the corner of her apron up and . . . ugh!

He wrested his imagination away from infant mothers and tried concentrating on the problem that faced him. The cemetery at midnight. Half an hour later his fertile imagination had come up with a solution. The tables were going to be turned on Kelly Ann and Monaghan. They were sending him into a cemetery to be frightened out of his wits. Well, he would come walking out of that same cemetery and frighten them out of what little wits they had between them!

It was 11:30 P.M. As he slipped out of bed and got dressed, Jamie could hear the sound of a late television program from the living room downstairs. Checking his special equipment he put it carefully into a paper bag and pocketed it. He could be back by half past midnight with any luck, plenty of time before the late movie finished and his father locked up for the night. As he stole past the living room doorway he could hear his mother. Dad would either be dozing or engrossed in the film, but that made little difference to the talking machine as she gabbled on, trying to get an Olympic

34

gold chattering medal and gab the opposition to death in the bargain.

"Goodness knows why you have to keep smoking that filthy old pipe! I have to get up early every morning, just to spray air freshener around this room before breakfast. It's bad for your health. I wonder why they keep showing that same commercial over and over. Why don't they get on with the film? Then decent people could get to their beds earlier, instead of watching how Antibiactosuds wash ten times cleaner than any other laundry detergent. If you keep walking on the backs of your slippers like that you'll ruin them, and fall and break your neck too."

Jamie closed the front door softly, made sure the side window was unlatched for his return, and padded across the lawn. As he jumped the hedge and set off down the road he felt much easier in his mind, now that he had a plan set to confound Monaghan and Kelly Ann. They were waiting for him at the cemetery gates. Monaghan emerged from the shadows.

"Okay, are you ready?"

"Of course I am."

Kelly Ann was unusually quiet. Jamie could not resist a dig at her.

"Huh! You look a bit scared."

"Not half as scared as you'll be, sitting next to a vampire's tomb at midnight."

"Yah! Vampires don't bother me a bit."

"Don't they? We'll see."

Jamie felt nervous and excited, but not fearful, as he climbed over the heavy black wrought-iron gates. Monaghan stated the conditions. "Right, fifteen minutes altogether. Ten minutes sitting on the step, and five minutes allowed for getting to and from the tomb. Go!"

A half moon hung in the sky amid scudding clouds; the slight breeze swayed bushes, making dim shadow patterns shimmer across the gravel path. Jamie clenched his fists, willing his feet to move steadily forward, one in front of the other. White stone angels appeared to be watching him with sightless eyes from between the serried rows of crosses and granite headstones; a heavy cloud momentarily obscured the moon. Jamie admitted it silently to himself: there was no doubt at all, he was frightened now. So frightened that he could not bring himself to turn his head and look back to the gates where Monaghan and Kelly Ann stood watching him.

No matter how carefully he tried to walk, the gravel crunched noisily underfoot. He chanced a quick look back, but all he saw was the yellow light from a street lamp across the road from the cemetery. When he turned back again he was forced to blink rapidly to dispel the bright reflections of the light from his vision. Jamie stumbled off the path, tripping on a cornerstone. Picking himself up, hopping about rubbing at his grazed knee, and staggered sideways into a bush.

Fffrrrrrtttttt!

Jamie yelped and sprang backwards as a blackbird, disturbed from its rest, fluttered off low into the night. Gritting his teeth he made himself plod doggedly onward to where the foreign graves stood.

Bong! Bong! Bong! Bong!

The church bell tolled out the midnight hour as he arrived trembling at his destination.

The green-bronze door of the tomb loomed cold and forbidding in the moonlight. Wind sighed mournfully through the rhododendron bushes and clouds blew across the night sky like the shrouds torn from long ago corpses. Jamie walked to the steps, trying to keep his mind off the next ten minutes by carrying out the first part of his plan. The thought of revenge upon the pair outside the gates settled his nerves somewhat. Seating himself on the vault steps he pulled out the crumpled paper bag, mentally counting to six hundred as he applied the makeup. Damping his face slightly, Jamie dabbed white flour heavily across his features, even right up into his hairline; the wind blew a bit away, but there was plenty left on him. He chuckled softly to himself as he imagined walking back down the path toward them in about eight minutes' time. Rolling yellow clay into two small stubby cones he affixed them to the side of his neck. Carefully he ringed the cones with purple felt-tip pen and dripped some of his mother's red food coloring beneath the two imitation vampire fang bites. About six minutes left to go now. Jamie smeared black rings around his eyes with some mascara he had borrowed from his mother's dressing table and used some dark blue eyeliner on his lips for the finishing touch. He shone a pencil light on his face as he made some final adjustments in his mother's compact mirror, tittering at the dreadful apparition he could see in the glass. Golly! Would they run when he came staggering and moaning at them.

The bronze door at his back began creaking and groaning as it started to open.

Hairs on the back of Jamie's neck stood up rigid. The blood in his veins turned to ice water; his heart pounded madly like a trip hammer, trying to fight its way up into his mouth. A pale bluish light radiated from the tomb, illuminating his quaking form. The hand that grasped Jamie's shoulder was neither big nor hairy, but it was as cold as iron in a blizzard, white and slim with a strength not of this earth. The green fingernails with their blackened edges dug unmercifully into his flesh as he was pulled to his feet. All strength and will drained from Jamie's body as the hand turned him forcefully to face the open door of the vault.

In the light from the grave Jamie saw he was face to face with a boy of his own age. His horrified eyes took in the strange boy's evil appearance. He was dressed in a long, flowing dark cape, fastened at the neck by a scarlet silk cord. His face was whiter than new-fallen snow. The boy's cruelly thin grey lips drew back, revealing a pair of sharp amber-colored fangs. His eyes had no whites, they were blazing red like some savage animal.

Jamie went completely stiff with terror as the vampire boy seized him by the hair, twisting his head agonizingly back to reveal the taut pulsating skin of his neck. Licking his lips with a black serpentine tongue, the vampire leered with devilish satisfaction at his petrified victim. Totally paralyzed, Jamie smelled vampire breath—musty, sweet, like long-dead flowers—as the needlelike fangs drew close to his unprotected neck.

"Yaaareeegh! Vladimir!"

Suddenly a huge female vampire sprang from the tomb and hurled Jamie bodily into the bushes. His eyes, wide with fear, were riveted on the scene before him. The large female gripped the boy vampire firmly by his waxlike pointed ear and shook him fiercely.

"Vladimir! What have I told you about drinking stale blood. Can't you see that the filthy little wretch has already been bitten by another vampire—look at the marks on his neck. You don't know what you could catch off him, sucking on an infected neck. Disgusting! That's what comes of hanging about with that gang of werewolves in the woods. Just wait till your father wakes up, my lad, he'll have a thing or two to say to you. I know you're only a hundred and fifty years old, but you should have more sense. Hell below! Just look at the mess of this good cape. Stand still while I brush it."

She turned upon Jamie with glittering eyes.

"And you! Get yourself off and die somewhere else, go on! Don't let me catch you haunting around this cemetery. And keep away from my Vladimir. He comes from a proper stone tomb with a bronze door, not just any old common grave. Be off with you!"

Jamie stumbled along the gravel path, the female vampire's wails drifting behind him on the night wind.

"You're a disgrace to the family, young Vlad. You can forget any fancy ideas of vacation in Transylvania this year. Look at those teeth, they're almost white. Stand still while I put some green on them from this vault door. Have you studied any bat flying lately? No, I'll bet you haven't. Well you can just stay in the tomb tonight and do some homework. . . ."

Monaghan peered through the wrought iron gates, trying hard to see along the gravelled path. Behind him Kelly Ann gnawed at a hangnail, her voice almost a sob.

"It's more than twenty minutes since he went in. Can you see him coming yet? What'll we say to his mother if he doesn't show up?"

Monaghan held up a hand to silence her. He watched intently for several minutes before turning to Kelly Ann, his face a picture of bewilderment.

"Yeah, I can see him now, trying to scrub some kind of mess off his face. He's sitting on a gravestone halfway down the path. . . . I think he's gone crazy, he seems to be chatting away to a stone angel!"

39

"What's he saying?"

"Dunno, can't quite hear him."

Kelly Ann tugged Monaghan roughly away from the gate.

"Here, I'll find out what he's talking about."

She forced her head through a wide space in the ironwork, and leaning to one side, she listened intently. Monaghan thrust his hands deep in his pockets, shuffling impatiently.

"Well, can you hear him? What's he saying?"

"He keeps laughing a lot and saying the same thing over and over. Now I'm *sure* he's gone loony."

"Never mind that, tell me what he's saying, will you!"

"Well, when he's not laughing all he says is, 'Just like my mother, just like my mother!'"

3

Always remember that if you're lucky
you'll live to be old one day.
It's not always the good who die young,
as I've heard people say.
One day your eyes won't be so bright,
your hearing won't be so good;
and winter cold will make you feel
the thinning of your blood.
So be kind to the old ones;
try to help them when you can.
Insure against your own old age,
young lady or young man.
Now here's a girl to read about,
who thinks she's not to blame,
because she's christened Alma
and she doesn't like her name.
She plays a game with old ones,
Alma, Allie. Who is who?
Dear reader, are you puzzled?
Good! My tale will interest you.

Allie Alma

Alma Budleigh detested her name. She did not like her surname Budleigh, and her christian name Alma she positively hated. It was flat-sounding, old-fashioned, horrible. Why inflict it on a girl, just because a great grandmother's aunt had been christened after some silly battle in the Crimean War hundreds of years ago? Was that a reason for a person to go through life saddled with a name like Alma? She insisted that everyone call her Allie, the girls at school, her friends, and the members of the Neighborhood Volunteer Help Junior Branch. Of course, there was little she could do to stop grownups, parents, teachers and the rest of adult society calling her Alma. They did not realize Allie was a different girl; Allie was lively, helpful and willing. However, Allie had a secret that nobody knew: she was a thief!

Mid-morning sunlight penetrated the drawn curtains of her bedroom, turning it into a pink grotto. Allie sprawled on the bed, clad in jeans and her NVHJB sweater. She emptied her treasures out of a resealable salad box onto the flowered quilt and handled them lovingly. There was Mrs. Carmichael's slim silver fobwatch, Miss Middleton's cloisonné pillbox, Mrs. Salten's eternity ring, Mrs. Bowden's amethyst brooch, Nannie Davidson's tortoiseshell barrette and Miss Blanchard's enamelled compact.

Allie breathed mist on the compact, polishing it against her pillowcase; A.B., the initials, shone brightly. How clever of Miss Alice Blanchard; fancy going to all the trouble of taking a trip to Edinburgh in 1952, just to buy a compact with both their initials engraved upon it. Allie thought of the game she played with her old ladies; it never failed to work. She popped Mrs. Salten's eternity ring on her little finger and admired it—the diamonds turned pink in the bedroom sunlight, the rubies an even deeper red. Surprisingly for such a valuable item, the game had been very easy.

"What are you looking for, Mrs. Salten? Can I help?"

"It's my eternity ring, dear. I always keep it in the little toby jug on the mantelpiece. I'm sure that's where I put it."

"Your eternity ring, you mean the beautiful little one with rubies and diamonds? We were looking at it only yesterday, weren't we?"

"Yes, dear, that's what I told myself this morning. I'm certain that I put it back in the jug, about five minutes before you left to go back to the Community Center."

"I don't remember seeing you put it back. Perhaps it was after I left that you put it in the jug."

"Hmm, maybe you're right, Alma, but I'm sure I put it back in the toby jug. I distinctly remember doing that."

"Which one, this jug or the one on the other side of the clock?"

"No, I only keep a few hairpins in that one. I'm positive it was the other one, that one you have your hand on."

Allie tried to frown and look sympathetic at the same time. It was difficult, but Allie was good at that sort of thing.

"Don't worry, Mrs. Salten, we'll find it. Now, let's look at this logically—you say you put it back in the jug just after I left."

"Did I, dear, I don't know what I'm saying today. It's all very upsetting, you know. Poor dear Lucy. It

43

was her ring; it's the only thing I have to remember my sister by."

Suddenly Allie clicked her fingers and smiled broadly. She watched the lights of hope dawn behind Mrs. Salten's harlequin-framed glasses.

"Of course, I remember now—"

"Remember what, dear?"

"You still had the ring on your finger when I left! Yes, I can recall taking your cup and saucer from you to wash them. You were sitting in that very chair, leaning back. Now try to think, what did you do next?"

"Well, er, let me see, had my afternoon nap I suppose. But I'm almost sure I put the ring in that jug."

Allie clasped Mrs. Salten's thin veined hand warmly.

"No no, I can see it clear as ever now. I let myself out and as I closed the door I looked back to see you were all right. I could distinctly see the ring on your thumb, hanging loosely. You said that it was far too big to fit any of your fingers, remember?"

"Oh yes, I did say that, didn't I?"

Allie stood with hands on hips, knowing that she looked the picture of a typically sensible and friendly young helper.

"Do you know what we're going to do? You and I are going to search down the sides of that armchair, under the cushions, shake the covers out, look under the rug by the chair. Thoroughly. I'm not leaving this house while you're still so unhappy about some silly old ring that doesn't even fit you. Come on now, Mrs. Salten, up you get!"

Allie began playing the game she had played many times before.

"Was the ring in the jewelry box upstairs?

"Had it slipped off into the tea caddy or the milk jug?

44

"What about the pockets of that cardigan you had on yesterday?

"Let's empty the vacuum cleaner out. Maybe it's in the bag?"

They did everything short of calling in a man to dismantle the armchair, which Mrs. Salten wouldn't hear of because it was her late husband's chair, and besides, workmen were so clumsy these days, the chair might get broken beyond repair. "They don't make furniture like that anymore, and things are so expensive these days, especially for a pensioner like me. . . ."

And so the game that Allie played expertly continued.

It always ended up the same. The old lady cried bitterly and Allie wept with her at the loss of the eternity ring.

"Oh, Mrs. Salten, please don't cry. I've got some money in my school savings bank. I'll draw it out on Tuesday and we'll look around the antique shops together. I'm sure we'll come across one just like it. Oh dear, d'you suppose seven pounds fifty pence will get us a good one?"

Mrs. Salten dried Allie's eyes and stroked her hair.

"Sssh, hush now, child, don't fret yourself over an old lady's keepsake. One day I'll probably come across it in the most unlikely place—when you grow old your mind plays tricks on you. Stop crying now and run along to your Community Center. You're a good girl, Alma. I won't forget how you've helped me."

Allie tugged a clump of lilac from an overhanging bush as she jogged up the avenue. It was a fact, Alma was a good girl. But Allie, well she was a different proposition.

"Alma, are you going to the Center today?"

Mrs. Budleigh's voice interrupted her daydream. Tumbling from the bed Allie scooped her treasures back into the box and resealed it. Swiftly removing the firescreen she tucked the box up onto a hidden chimney ledge as she called out, "Coming, Mum, won't be a moment."

At the Community Center Allie produced her Volunteer Helpers (Junior Branch) card, and watched as Geoff Philips wrote carefully on it with his executive fibertip pen. He winked broadly at her as he handed the card back. "We could do with more like you, young lady. In fact I wish we had a hundred little Almas running around helping our senior citizens."

Allie shuddered inwardly as Alma smiled outwardly.

"Thanks, Mr. Philips. Dad said to tell you he'd be at the golf club tomorrow if you fancy a game."

Geoff pulled a mock sad face.

"Lucky old Dad, eh? As for me, it'll be some time yet before we've cleaned up that section of the canal so that fish can swim in it again. You tell your dad that it's thigh boots and mud for me, not golf clubs and Scotch. Oh, by the way, the lady you're visiting, Mrs. Struben, she's from Austria. You may have a bit of trouble trying to understand her."

Alma smiled shyly. "Oh I expect I'll manage, Mr. Philips. Bye now."

"Have a nice day, Alma."

She breezed through the swing doors into the car park. "I don't know about Alma," she whispered to herself, "but Allie's in for a very nice day, Geoff."

Fourteen D Ferryview Towers was on the fourth floor. Allie's eyes roved about the apartment, and she decided it looked quite promising. Mrs. Struben read the details from the Junior Helpers card in her quaint accent. "Elma Budligg from zer Volunteers Helpen, ach so!"

When they had got it established that Alma Budleigh was the correct pronunciation and Shtrooben was the way you say Struben, Alma began writing down the old lady's shopping list. Mrs. Struben was very fond of chocolate and coffee, which she called "Schokolade und Kaffee." Apart from that her needs were quite modest: powdered milk, margarine, soup and cereal. Alma wrote the list as Allie cast secret glances over Mrs. Struben's possessions.

Then Allie spotted the egg!

It perched in the top of a candlestick, like a golf ball sitting on a tee. The egg was hinged; there was bound to be something of interest inside such a curio. Allie decided that she wanted it.

When she returned from the store with the old lady's groceries there were dishes to wash and further instructions from Mrs. Struben on her likes and dislikes.

"Ven you go to der schoppen, Elma, remember I use der packet soup, not canned, also I like the softer margareen."

After Alma had dusted around they sat down to coffee and cookies. Allie decided on the first moves of the game, half listening to Mrs. Struben. She was not from Vienna, she came from a city in Germany called Cologne and was very proud of the fact. She told Alma of her life before the war, as Allie took care to laugh in all the right places and shake her head sympathetically at the sad parts of the story. She looked intently at faded photographs of generations of Strubens and gasped in feigned amazement at the tales of the terrible war.

Gradually they got around to the items of interest in

47

the living room. Allie took great care to show only a passing curiosity as the old lady prattled on from one thing to another.

"Elma, you see this fine pipe, it is called a meerschaum. It belonged to mein papa, he was a railway engineer, you know."

"It's a very nice pipe. What's this scent called?"

"Ah, der Kölnichwasser, how you say . . . Eau de Cologne. It comes from mein city. I think it is der nicest fragrant in der world. I was given it for mein name day, you know, like your birthday."

"Oh I see. Well you do have some nice things here, Mrs. Struben. What's this little bottle called?"

"Dat is schnapps, very gut. Mein bruder, he would bring this home from Munich; he vas a student in college there."

"Yes, my father has a collection of miniature whiskey bottles, just like this one. Did this egg belong to your brother?"

Mrs. Struben half turned in her chair as Allie lifted the egg from its perch on the candlestick.

"Be careful, Elma, don't drop it, child! Bring it here, I vill show you."

Allie sat on the arm of Mrs. Struben's chair as the old lady opened the tiny brass clasp. "See, Elma, this vas mein family."

Her hands trembled as she gently parted the hinged egg. Inside was a detail in fine miniature, exquisitely carved. Four adults and three children sat around a table in a small room. Amazingly there was a copy of the egg, almost microscopic, set in the middle of the table. The entire structure was fashioned from papier-mâché and matchsticks, lovingly painted in painstaking detail. Allie was even more certain now that it would be hers.

Mrs. Struben related the story of the egg. "I haf always lived in apartments. In 1941 we were living in a ground-floor apartment, not far from der Neumarkt area of Cologne. There vas my father and mother, my elder brother, my Uncle Wolfgang, Aunt Kirsten and their daughter Helga. The war vas horrible. Each night der planes would fly over and bomb our beautiful city. Mother always worried over Papa; der railway stations and train lines suffered greatly during the bombing raids; ve vould kneel and pray each night dat Papa got home safe. My bruder had to finish with college because of der war; mother vas afraid that he vould be taken to serve in the army. However, he vas sent to work in a civilian job, filling out forms in government offices. Uncle Wolfgang vas a jeweler and a fine goldsmith. He had lost a leg in der first great war, so the army had no further use for him.

"Everywhere there vas shortages, food vas scarce, fuel hard to come by, and new clothing out of the question. However, Mother and Aunt Kirsten always made ends meet for us somehow.

"Each morning I would go out to school with mein cousin Helga; she vas the same age as me, fifteen years. We would see der scars and wreckage of der last night's bombings, der post office gone, der park wrecked. All around there vas heaps of rubble, with people digging in debris for the remains of their loved ones. It vas a frightening time to be a young girl growing up in Cologne. One morning my uncle's shop was bombed, he could no longer work there. Die air raids had become so frequent that Papa moved us into der basement room of our apartment house.

"Der sound of bombs falling ist something you cannot imagine. First there ist a whistling noise from far

49

off; it grows louder and louder until you think it ist going straight through your head. Suddenly there is a loud bang! Your ears ring, der walls shake, der lights flicker on und off; glass windows shatter into fragments und you are covered in dust from Gott knows where. This is gut. It means you are still alive, the bomb did not drop on your home, you are lucky, someone else ist dead, their home is now only a hill of rubble. And on and on it vent, every night.

"Christmas 1941 der food vas extra scarce, but Papa's train struck a hare by accident and killed it. We had meat! Mother and Aunt Kirsten prepared a wonderful Christmas meal from dat hare und some other things they had saved from the rations. Helga und I made a crib with the Christ child in it. My bruder sang 'O Tannenbaum' and played on his guitar. It vas a small island of joy in the middle of misery. Uncle Wolfgang made gifts for us all; he vas very clever with his hands. To mein papa he gave a little shield with our City arms painted on it. Mein mother und aunt received an embroidered handkerchief each; to my bruder he gave a soft leather case for his glasses, and mein cousin Helga was given a pair of handmade slippers from her father. I vas his special favorite, though, and he gave me this egg. 'See, Anna,' he said. 'Here is our little family sitting in this basement, safe within an egg. If you keep this with you no harm will befall us.' I think mein cousin Helga was not happy with her slippers. She would gaze at my egg a lot; I would not let her play with it und she wept. Uncle Wolfgang told her not to be silly, but Helga wanted mein egg. She stared and stared at it, as if it had been made for *her*. The egg vas much nicer than Helga's slippers, und it vas mine.

"Der very next night the bombs began falling as they had never done. Massive explosions shook der whole city. Houses, apartments, whole buildings full of living souls who had never done harm to anyone were wiped out. It vas as if a giant foot had come out of the sky and stamped upon them. We huddled in the corner of der basement, clinging to each other. Outside der roar und clatter of death continued, mingled with der screams of the wounded und dying. Bombs do not care who they drop on. The next thing we heard vas the klaxon horn blaring out in der street. Air raid wardens, firemen, and police were herding folk into trucks und vehicles.

" 'Come out, leave your homes, the whole district is being flattened. Hurry, we will take you to the countryside where it is safer.'

"We listened to the men shouting outside as we crouched in a corner, too scared to move. Mein papa and Uncle Wolfgang began urging us to leave. I can still hear Papa shouting to my mother over der noise of the air raid.

" 'Schnell, schnell! Leave everything, take the children and get out!'

"There vas a mighty bang! Der basement windows vere blown out, frames and all; ve began screaming in panic. Papa pushed Uncle Wolfgang out of der basement window, and he started reaching in to help us out. A truck loaded with families vas hit, bodies lay everywhere, and the vehicles started to drive away. I dropped der egg. It rolled back down into der cellar, and Helga scrambled back down after it.

"I vas frightened, but angry too. I tried going in after her, but Papa held me back.

" 'It is mine. Uncle Wolfgang made the egg for me!' I screamed at him.

51

"Papa stroked my hair. 'Helga will get it for you, liebling.'

"I struggled to get free from Papa. 'Nein, nein, she wants it for herself!'

"*Bang*!

"A bomb struck the street and hit a main gas pipe. The whole area vas lit up by a blue and white light. I vas flung against der wall, unconscious.

"It vas daylight when I came to. A fireman vas wiping my face; I was still alive, though I don't know how. Papa too, and Mother, we had been saved by some sort of miracle. Uncle Wolfgang and Aunt Kirsten were hugging each other and sobbing. They kept trying to go to der basement, but the wardens would not let them. Do you know what, der basement vas still unharmed—the bombs, explosions und falling rubble had not touched it. A fireman and a helper carried der body of mein cousin Helga out into the street. In her hand she still held mein lovely egg. I felt so ashamed, but I took it from her, because it was mine.

"The fireman said dat Helga vas dead, not from any injury, but from shock. The fright of being crouched alone in the basement without any of her family when the bomb hit the gas main, it had stopped the poor girl's heart. There was no other explanation."

Alma sat stunned by the dreadful tale.

Allie had heard none of it, she was gazing greedily at the egg.

Four days later the game started in earnest.

"Mrs. Struben, I remembered to get packet soup instead of the canned, though there's no soft margarine in until tomorrow. I'll put these things away and then we'll have a nice cup of coffee. Mrs. Struben, what's the matter?"

"Elma, mein egg is gone!"

"Egg, what egg? There's eggs in the fridge."

"Nein, nein, the egg mein uncle made for me in Köln."

"There there now, don't get so upset. I can hardly understand you when you get yourself in a state like this."

"But it vas here only this morgen, mein egg. It's gone, I'm telling you!"

"Look, let's sit down and discuss this thing sensibly over coffee. Eggs can't walk, you know. Don't worry, we'll find it."

And so the game went on to its inevitable conclusion.

Leaving 14D Ferryview Towers Allie had a film of perspiration on her brow. Goodness knows how Alma would have handled that one—it had taken all of Allie's skill, but she had won. They had argued and searched, debated and scoured the apartment from end to end, then argued some more. At one point Mrs. Struben came right out with it and accused her of stealing the egg. Alma got really frightened, but Allie didn't; she gambled on a risky hunch that paid off well. Allie said she was going to phone for the police.

The old lady had become even more upset. She had an unreasoning terror of uniformed authority— well, perhaps not unreasoning, having lived in Nazi Germany.

"Nein, nein, Elma, not der polizei please, liebchen!"

It had all ended successfully. Allie cried until her face was red and puffy, offered to help from her meager school savings, accepted a tearful apology from Mrs. Struben and left with her now practiced farewell.

"Don't worry, Mrs. Struben, your egg will turn up.

It's only a question of time. You'll probably find it in the least likely place, somewhere we wouldn't have dreamed of looking."

That night Allie lay in bed, thinking of her growing treasure stowed away in the box on the chimney ledge. The egg made a beautiful addition to her collection. Sleep did not come easily that night, but in the end dull old Alma took over and wafted her off to dreamland.

She slept for only a short time. Allie woke with a start, the noise in her dreams forcing her up to the surface of wakefulness. And the noise was still there now that she was wide awake, rumbling, roaring, whistling, screaming, crashing.

At first Allie thought it must be an old war movie on the television downstairs—her father often sat up late to watch such things. Half reassured, she lay back and tried to recapture sleep. That was when the noise grew louder and the dust began choking her mouth and nostrils.

Then the bombs started to drop. She could hear the whistle from far away overhead, getting closer. Both Allie and Alma lay rigid, petrified; the whole world seemed to be exploding. Allie managed to lift her hand, protecting her eyes from the grit and dust that was raining from the ceiling. Fear rose in her mouth, a sour-tasting bile, mixing with the dirt and powdered glass. Each time a bomb dropped Allie thought it was a direct hit. She tried to scream but no sound came from her constricted throat. She was all alone; Alma had gone, deserted her. Through a space in her fingers she saw the walls of the little basement room shake with each explosion; the group of matchstick people seated around the table, wooden, impassive, as outside the skies rained down death. Planes droned overhead, klaxons and sirens blared outside. Allie's world was transformed into an Armageddon of fire, smoke, dust and choking rubble.

A gigantic bang shook the entire room. She could see the windows and frames had been blasted out, the matchstick folk who had sat at the table were no longer there.

"Elma, where are you?"

"Allie, please come out!"

Clawing hands of blue and white flame lit up the scene with an unearthly radiance. Allie shrunk against the wall, crouching there like a trapped animal, her mouth wide open in a silent scream that would not come forth. Two massive faces peered in through the burning window space – it was Alma and Mrs. Struben. They called to her over the roar of death and carnage.

"Come out, Allie, oh please come out!"

"Elma, bring mein egg to me!"

They called louder and louder as Allie shrank further back into the basement. Suddenly the bombing stopped, the voices faded, and there was darkness and peace. Allie felt herself floating on a silent black sea of infinity.

The full staff of the Neighborhood Volunteer Help Junior Branch attended the service, as did some of the old people they served: Mrs. Carmichael, Miss Middleton, Mrs. Salten, Nannie Davidson, Miss Alice Blanchard and Mrs. Struben.

"Such a dreadful thing to happen suddenly to a young girl."

"Indeed, one expects it to happen with folk of our age, but a young teenager dying of a heart attack. Dreadful!"

"But was it a heart attack, dear? I heard they said it was natural causes, for want of something better."

"Well, whatever it was it's a crying shame, poor young thing."

"Hmm, I had a cousin who died just like that long ago in der war. I think it was greed that killed her. But dat was many long years ago. Aah mein poor Elma, no wait, it vas Helga. I get mixed up, you know, Helga, Elma, all so long ago. . . ."

4

Satan, the Devil, Beelzebub, Old Nick,
he's always ready when we find good,
to work some wicked trick.
What is truth, where is it at?
Don't dare ask Henry Mawdsley that!
It comes to me as no surprise,
that Henry Mawdsley always lies.
Truth to Henry Mawdsley is like a hot ice cream.
Truth to Henry Mawdsley is just a passing dream.
Truth to Henry Mawdsley is a sausage that has legs.
Truth to Henry Mawdsley is a bunny rabbit's eggs.
Truth to Henry Mawdsley is a chunk of lead to bounce.
Truth to Henry Mawdsley is the ton that weighs an ounce.
Truth to Henry Mawdsley is an undiscovered beast.
Truth to Henry Mawdsley is the North Pole, pointing East.
Ask anyone in all the world, they'll tell you with a sigh,
"Even when he's fast asleep, Henry has to lie!"

The Lies of Henry Mawdsley

They said Henry Mawdsley was an inveterate liar; sometimes they said he was an habitual liar; more often than not they said he was a born liar. Henry liked that last one; he chuckled at the thought of himself at the tender age of one week, standing up in his cot to spout out fibs at his amazed parents.

Henry was very proud of being a liar—not everyone could tell good lies; it took practice. All those years of learning to keep a straight face while telling a totally fictitious saga, of trying to look completely truthful while telling an untruth—not easy. However, Henry had taken to his chosen calling like a dog to a string of pork sausages.

Folk who did not know him were inclined to believe his lies. What irked Henry was that those who knew him also knew not to believe him—teachers, parents, school friends and neighbors, and people of that ordinary everyday honest ilk. In fact, the longer Henry Mawdsley lived and the more people he got to know, the less his fictitious fables were apt to be believed.

Until the day that Henry Mawdsley met the Devil.

Truth to tell, it was not a dramatic encounter by any stretch of the imagination. Henry was sitting on a park bench one morning, late for school as usual. Deep in his lying heart even Henry had to admit he was not the world's most successful student. To him math was a mystery, biology was a bafflement, and a single page of the English written word appeared to his eyes as some obscure Sanskrit squiggle. Like a drowning man to a straw Henry grasped at any excuse to avoid education; trouble was, he had used up every excuse several times. Scuffing the gravel path alongside the bench Henry dug among his mental store of wild untruths, trying to think up a suitable whopper. His mind had latched on to the old blazing house fire story, in which he rescued a small infant whose parents had taken so long weeping upon his shoulder and congratulating him that the whole incident made him late for school. If Mrs. Benson (Henry's teacher) did not believe him, then she could look for herself in the evening papers, where it would probably be reported in banner headlines, unless the silly reporter forgot to put his story in.

The old man sitting at the opposite end of the bench nodded to him. "No school today, young fellow?"

Henry shook his head sadly.

"No, not today. They've found deathwatch beetles in the floors and ceilings; the place could collapse at any minute. I 'spect it'll be at least three years before the repairs are finished."

The old man pulled a lighted cigar from his overcoat pocket and puffed away reflectively. Henry tried not to show surprise as he asked the kindly looking old man, "How did you do that, with your cigar I mean?"

"Oh, just the odd bit of magic."

Henry nodded understandingly. "My father's a magician, you know."

The old gentleman raised his eyebrows at this remark.

"A magician, you say. What name does he go under?"

Henry kept his face straight. "Er, the Great Majikio."

"Hmm, I think I've heard of him. What's your name?"

"Tex Dangerfield," Henry lied. "What's yours?"

"Oh, nothing as romantic as yours, Tex, just plain old Nick Lucifer."

"Nick Lucifer, not a bad name for a magician. Can you teach me any tricks, Mr. Lucifer?"

"Why? Doesn't your father teach you any of his tricks?"

"Only one or two simple ones. He's gone off to Australia to do shows on TV for the eskimos over there. I haven't seen him for ten years or so."

Nick Lucifer tossed his cigar into the lake. It turned into a piece of bread and a passing duck gobbled it up.

"I might be able to teach you a trick or two, Tex, but how will you pay me for the lessons?"

Henry had to think about this for a moment.

"Now and then Dad sends me over some Australian money. He's got loads of it. It's called pesetas. I could give you some of that, any bank'll change it."

"Hmmm, Australian pesetas, I'm not so sure. Besides I've got all the money I need, I'm reasonably wealthy."

"Oh I see. What do you want then, Mr. Lucifer?"

The old man reached behind Henry's ear and pulled forth a scroll of old-fashioned-looking paper.

"I'd like your name on the bottom of this, Tex."

"My name, what for?"

Mr. Lucifer tipped his hat back upon his head. A small black horn showed; hurriedly he straightened the hat.

"It's called a Soul Ownership Form H, zero, T. After a week your soul belongs to me."

Henry brightened up. "Ha! So that's what Sole Ownership means. Like when I lose my math book in school, Mrs. Benson says that I must find it because I alone am responsible for Sole Ownership of my math book."

Nick Lucifer scratched the pointed lobe of his ear.

60

"Er, something like that, Tex, but this form actually states that your soul belongs to me after a week. It's got nothing to do with math books."

Henry was only half listening. Digging his hand into his coat pocket he tried to produce a lighted cigar, but the only thing he could come up with was a wad of fluff-covered chewing gum. That was good enough. He popped it into his mouth as if he had performed a marvelous trick.

"You want my soul?"

Nick Lucifer explained patiently. "Yes, your soul. It's not as if I'm taking something you can feel or see, like your football or skateboard. Look, tell me, have you ever felt, seen, or even heard your soul?"

Henry shook his head. "Can't say I have, but why d'you want it?"

Nick Lucifer produced a brimming glass of his favorite port wine from out of thin air, and sipped reflectively.

"You could call it a foolish old man's hobby, really. I'm a soul collector."

"Like stamps and beer coasters and that sort of thing?"

"Well, something like that. Is it a deal?"

Henry blew a bubble, half fluff, half gum. "What do I get out of it."

Nick Lucifer spread his arms expansively.

"The world, my boy, the world! But only for a week. You can be the world's greatest magician, the world champion skateboarder, whatever you wish. World boyweight boxing champion, brilliant concert pianist, world math wizard, anything at all."

Henry threw the bubble gum to the ducks. They ignored the sticky lump.

"Okay, give me a pen and I'll sign your Sole Ownership Form."

The old gentleman bounded from the bench with surprising agility. He did a handstand and landed in the middle of a clump of bushes.

"Come into my office, young man. This has got to be done properly."

Henry followed him into the bushes. Suddenly the ground yawned open, revealing a flight of stone steps; from the depths a purply-red light and yellow smoke emanated. Nick Lucifer smiled enticingly at his young friend.

"I'll bet you've never seen anything like this before."

Henry followed him nonchalantly down the winding stairway. "Of course I have. My Auntie Dollie had one of these in her back garden," he lied. "Uncle Al had to fill it in, though, 'cause her poodle kept falling down it."

Down, down they went, finally descending to a great underground cavern, with crimson flames shooting out of its rocky floor and great billows of yellow sulphur smoke belching from cracks in the walls. From somewhere the sound of a great organ playing fell upon Henry's astounded ears. He tried hard not to show astonishment and was about to mention that it sounded like his school song when Nick Lucifer silenced him by performing another amazing trick. He stamped his foot down hard and a huge rock table sprang up from the floor. He placed his glass of port upon it and spread the parchment ina businesslike way, pointing to a space at the bottom line.

"Sign right there, young man, but first listen carefully to what I have to say. Take this pen and pierce your fingertip; it must be signed in your own blood. Just a little scratch, it won't hurt you."

Henry snorted scornfully.

"You bet it won't. I've had my arm torn off in a car accident and sewed back on with microscope surgery. A scratch with some old pen, huh, that's nothing."

Nick Lucifer forgot himself for a moment and looked heavenward for patience. He continued speaking in a somewhat strained voice.

"As I was saying, it won't hurt, but you must sign your proper name at the bottom of the contract, Henry Mawdsley. Please don't insult my intelligence by signing Tex Dangerfield. You told me a little untruth there, didn't you?"

Henry was most indignant.

"Little untruth! I don't tell little untruths, Mr. Lucifer, I tell whopping good lies. I'm an expert at it. My motto is that I'd rather have a liar than a thief any day."

Handing Henry the pen, Nick Lucifer clapped him encouragingly on the back. "A boy after my own black heart. Sign and make your wish."

Henry swallowed rather nervously. "Just one thing, Mr. Lucifer."

"Yes Henry, what's that?"

"Well, I'd like a drink of your wine, I feel a bit nervous, y'see."

"Certainly m'boy, be my guest, drain the glass if you feel like it."

"No, just a sip, thanks. Oh, there is one other thing."

Nick Lucifer drummed his long clawlike nails impatiently on the table.

"What is it now, Henry?"

"I don't like the idea of sticking a pen into myself."

"Righto! Hold still, sonny, I'll do it for you."

Henry grasped the metal-nibbed pen tightly.

"No, no, I'll do it myself if you don't mind. But there is one other thing I'm not too happy about."

Nick Lucifer drummed his cloven feet against the floor in exasperation. Henry artfully concealed his surprise at the sight of them, whilst at the same time thinking it would be rather handy never to wear shoes or socks—the odd hoof trim might prove painful but Nick looked like he was made of stern stuff.

Flames roared high, smoke billowed heavily about them, mingled with tortured moans from somewhere far below. A trickle of smoke wisped from the old man's left ear. "Tell me, what is it now?"

"Well, it's the sight of my own blood, or even the thought of someone else watching me stick pens into myself. Look, I'm sorry, but I think we'd better forget the whole thing."

The sound of Nick Lucifer's teeth grinding together was like a knife scraping across a polished dinner plate.

"You can't back out now, boy. Surely you want to be the greatest something or other in the world for a whole week?"

Henry Mawdsley's eyes were childishly meek.

"Of course I'd like to, Mr. Lucifer. But both you and I would see the pen stick into my skin and warm red blood oozing out; it'd be worse than getting an injection at the hospital. I feel quite faint at the thought of it. You should too."

Nick Lucifer tried hard to fix a kindly smile on his strained face.

"Listen, Henry, I've got an idea. How would it be if I cloaked us both in heavy smoke? That way neither of us would see your blood oozing out. You could call out once you've done it. How's that?"

Henry smiled charmingly. "Thank you, Mr. Lucifer. How good of you."

Good? The look on Nick Lucifer's face would have stopped clocks. He drew in his breath and blew out: a thick impenetrable fog of yellow sulphur smoke enveloped them both.

"Come on, come on, get it done, Henry. Now!"

"Yowch! Aahh, that hurt!"

"Is your finger pierced, boy?"

"I'll say it is! And it hurt like the devil."

Immediately the smoke cleared to reveal Henry Mawdsley sucking furiously on his forefinger. Nick Lucifer laughed happily.

"Don't be a big baby. Hurry up now and sign the paper."

Henry flourished the pen. "I'm prob'ly the best signature writer in all my school, y'know."

Nick Lucifer drained the port wine and chewed the glass into fragments with temper.

"Yes, yes, get on with it, will you. Get on with it!"

Henry hovered, the pen a fraction away from the parchment.

A long tail burst forth through the back of Nick Lucifer's overcoat. It lashed back and forth savagely. "Sign, blast you, sign!"

Henry nodded in admiration of the tail trick.

"Oh, righto. Now let me see, what'll I be? The world's greatest fiddle player . . . no. Greatest magician in the world? Hmmm, no. I could always write off to Dad for more tricks—"

Nick Lucifer's eyes had turned bright red. They popped out like organ stops. "Sign! Sign!"

Henry paused, smiling with satisfaction.

"I know! Could I have people to entirely believe all I say for a week? Y'see, I'm the world's best liar, like I told you, but it's hard when people don't believe me.

Mr. Lucifer, can you fix it so that everyone believes every word I say for a week?"

Nick Lucifer was already long past the end of his tether. He grabbed a three-pronged trident out of the air and dashed at Henry, screaming aloud, "Anything! Anything! Sign! Yaaaah!"

Noticing that Mr. Lucifer seemed upset Henry put pen to paper and signed. Hardly had he made his final flourish when the old gent seized the scroll and thrust it deep into his pocket.

"Wait, Mr. Lucifer, it might smudge. Perhaps I'd better blow on it to dry it out for you and make it nice and neat."

Nick Lucifer was dancing around insanely. Flames and sulphur jets shot high, rocks cracked thunderously, green molten fluid gushed from ragged cracks in the walls, the sound of tortured souls below rose to an anguished wail. Mr. Lucifer did look peculiar.

"Get out of my sight, wretched and damned boy. Out, before I blast you into eternity!"

Remembering his manners, Henry handed the pen back.

"I've never been blasted into eternity, though I did stow away on a space shuttle once and nearly got blasted to Neptune—"

The hat flew from Nick Lucifer's head; his two devilish horns writhed and wriggled as they extended from his satanic skull. This seemed to calm him a bit, for he pointed his trident at Henry and spoke in a deep hellish official boom.

"Your wish is granted, Henry Mawdsley. Whatsoever you say will be believed by all mankind for the space of one week. But when midnight of the seventh day strikes, I will arise from the pit of Eblis,

66

from the flames of Hades, from the inferno of torment, to claim your soul. Now begone!"

There followed the usual bangings and whooshings and Henry Mawdsley found himself back above ground in the bushes. There was no sign of fiery caverns gaping in the earth, or of Mr. Lucifer. "Hoi! What d'you think you're doing in there. Come out at once." Henry emerged to confront the park policeman. Now was the time to try out his new powers.

"Good morning, Constable. I'm trying to find the math book that the wind blew out of my hands. It's called *Math for the Mathematical* by Professor Henry Mawdsley, but I can't find it and I'm already late for school, you see."

The policeman made a note of the name in his notebook.

"Don't worry, sir, you get right along to your school. Leave it to me, I'll find it for you. Oh, which school shall I deliver it to?"

"Olympia Avenue Primary Juniors, please. Just mention my name—Sebastian Twinklefurt the Third."

Noting the name down, the policeman saluted cheerily to Henry.

"Right you are, Mr. Twinklefurt. Have a nice day, sir."

It worked!

Henry Mawdsley smiled a grin of pure fiendish delight as he strolled schoolward, late as usual.

Mr. Taylor the principal was about to collect some exam papers from his car in the car park when he spied Henry ambling coolly across the sports field.

"You, boy, come here immediately!"

Mr. Taylor consulted his watch sternly.

"Twenty minutes past ten, lad. Are you aware of what time school starts?"

Henry smiled disarmingly. "Half past ten, sir."

Mr. Taylor clapped his hands briskly. "Quite right. Nothing like being nice and early, eh. Run along now."

As Henry walked into class Mrs. Benson fixed him with an icy glare.

"Henry Mawdsley, how nice of you to honor us with your presence. You, the worst student in my class—you cannot read, write, spell, or solve the most elementary mathematical problem. But does that seem to bother you? It certainly does not! Your parents will hear about this, Mawdsley, strolling in here every day abysmally late without as much as a by your leave. Well, what's the excuse today, young man? Another house fire and a baby rescue?"

The entire class giggled. Henry Mawdsley was about to be condemned to a week's detention; he had long ago had his final warning.

Henry stood to attention and spoke out courageously.

"Mrs. Benson, I cannot tell a lie to you. I was on my way to school early today when I saw an old lady trapped high in a tree. She had climbed up there after her dear old tomcat and its six little kittens. Though heaven knows how they had got up there. Well, I immediately halted a passing bus and climbed onto its roof, from where I made a reckless leap, never thinking of my own safety, straight into the branches of the tree. It was so high that it took me over an hour to reach her. Using my shoelaces to strap her to my back, I filled all my pockets with the kittens, then, gripping the dear old tomcat tightly in my teeth, I climbed down. They are all safe at home and quite recovered now. It was the least I could have done."

68

The class applauded wildly. Mrs. Benson's lip quivered and she wiped her eyes on a lace handkerchief.

"Oh, you dear boy. Somebody get him a glass of water. Sit at my desk and rest yourself awhile, Henry Mawdsley. Such bravery, such devotion to an old lady and her pets. You must be exhausted."

Henry looked modestly at the floor.

"I am a bit shaken up; perhaps I'd better have the rest of the day off."

As the object of her affections sauntered homeward, Mrs. Benson set the class to making banners and posters for "Heroic Henry Week." They worked with burning enthusiasm, many of them blowing their noses noisily on the banners because they still felt very emotional.

Mrs. Mawdsley stood hands on hips, confronting her son. "Henry, have you dodged off school again?"

He sat his mother down in an armchair to prepare her for the news.

"I've been sent home, Mom. The school doctor examined me, and he said that perhaps I'd like to be alone, considering my condition."

Mrs. Mawdsley clutched a tea towel to her lips.

"Not headlice or verrucas. Tell me, Henry."

Henry shook his head despairingly.

"Goodylackosis. I may not last the week out."

His mother sobbed brokenly. "Oh, Henry, don't say that. Is there no cure at all for this Goodylackosis?"

"I don't know yet. What's for dinner?"

"Liver casserole, potatoes and string beans. Oh how can you think of food at a time like this, my brave little soldier?"

With forefinger and thumb Henry pinched the bridge

69

of his nose. He looked very intelligent.

"Got it! Liver casserole and all that stuff aren't goodies. Give them to Dad. Run down to the store quickly, we may yet be in time, Mother. Don't you see, it's goodies I need to fight off this illness, goodies! Get me some chocolate-fudge ice cream, a double chili cheeseburger, and whatever cans of cola you can lay your hands on. Oh, and a box of fresh cream eclairs and a jumbo butterscotch milkshake. Hurry!"

Mrs. Mawdsley dried her eyes and lunged for her shopping cart. "How clever of you, my little genius. Sit right there and watch TV until I get back. I'll be as quick as possible!"

Henry stretched out on the settee with the remote control as his mother clattered off like a runaway express train.

Good old Mr. Lucifer. Henry began thinking what fun his father would have doing lots of homework, because of his son's fractured wrist.

Five days had passed in which Henry Mawdsley revelled in his new-found powers. Taxi drivers conveyed him freely everywhere he wanted to go, merely at the mention of his sick granny. Sweetshops, soda fountains and pizza parlors threw open their doors wide to the poor boy who had not eaten for a month. The manager of the Palace Cinema kept the best seat in the house permanently vacant for Henry with his rare eye condition. An open-mouthed senior school football team sat riveted as Goal-line Mawdsley related his match-winning tactics. Once he even set the Townswomen's Guild atwitter, telling how he, Needles Mawdsley, had knitted a full two-tone house cover, complete with door and window flaps. There was not a

70

police patrol in town that would not have willingly relinquished its eyeteeth to have the latest hot bank robbery tipoff from Mawdlsey the Lip.

Late on the evening of the sixth day Henry was coming out of his local restaurant, full of chocolate-fudgecheesecreamburger (now the speciality of the house since Coolcat Mawdlsey had invented it) when he walked straight into the middle of a bunch of street-corner toughs. There were ten of them, and they tried the usual excuse to beat him up.

"C'mere, kid."

"Who, me?"

"Yeah, you. We don't like the way you're lookin' at us. D'you think you're funny or somethin'?"

"I'm Henry Mawdsley, of course I'm funny. Why did the chicken cross the road? To get to the other side, of course."

Henry swaggered off, leaving the would-be muggers doubled up on the pavement, tears streaming from their eyes as they held their ribs. "Hahahaohohohohee-heehee! To get to the other . . . hoohoohoo that's a good one. Why did the ch . . . hahahahaha!"

Henry Mawdsley sighed, a deep sound of boredom and frustration. Life had been much more rewarding when he was forced to work hard at making his lies believable. Now it was all too easy.

The vicar raised his hat respectfully as Henry slouched by the rectory gate.

"Good evening young man. How did your mission to the wilds of Ungamunga fare?"

The last thing Henry needed was a discussion with the vicar on bringing the good word to untamed regions of the world. He quickened his pace.

"Er, I converted all the Ungamungians, Vicar.

71

'Scuse me, I'm late for my flight. Just jetting off to sort that lot out in Cannibolia. Lots of heathens out there, y'know."

The reverend gentleman waved his Sunday sermon notes at the receding figure. "Fight the good fight, Henry. Keep up the splendid work, m'boy."

On the morning of the seventh day Henry Mawdsley had perked up considerably. He had lain late in bed thinking up a brilliant plan. Walter Furlong, his old archenemy, the dullest, most cynical boy in the whole of Olympia Avenue Primary Juniors, was the very fellow to try it out on. Henry flagged down a passing car and jumped in beside the driver, an old lady on her way to afternoon bingo.

"Olympia Avenue School, quickly! There's a foreign spy trying to get the exam papers from the principal's safe. I'm from the Secret Service."

The antiquated car screeched its way around into High Street, leaving a burning strip of rubber tire tread for twenty yards. Mrs. Kamenish clamped her hat on tight, making clicking noises with her dentures as she booted the accelerator, sending the needle hovering between eighty-five and ninety.

"Heehee! Don't worry, young feller. I drove an armored staff car all over Europe in World War Two, I'll get you there pronto!"

Pale and somewhat shaky Henry made his way to the gates, in time to see the pupils emerging for lunchtime recess. Walter was one of the last, his lips set in a perpetual sneer of disbelief as Henry walked alongside him.

"Walter, what would you say if I told you I was the world's biggest liar?"

Walter seated himself upon the school wall staring coldly at Henry. "I'd say you were correct, Mawdsley. You definitely are the biggest liar in the world. I've always known it."

Henry nodded in agreement as he warmed to his subject.

"And what would you say if I told you not to believe a single word from my mouth?"

"Then I certainly wouldn't."

"Honestly?"

"Cross my heart and hope to go bang if I do."

A tear of pure relief sprung from the corner of Henry's right eye. He stared happily into the scornful face of Walter Furlong. At last, here was someone who actually disbelieved him.

"Walter, you're an angel!"

No sooner were the words out when Walter dug a Frisbee from his schoolbag. Setting it on his head like a halo he leapt from the school wall, both hands joined devoutly, furiously flapping his shoulder blades together as if they were wings.

Henry clasped his head in his hands and cried bitterly.

"Do not weep, Henry, for I have come from heaven to comfort you."

Henry gritted his teeth. "Oh bug off, Walter, you stupid baboon."

"Whuh, whuh, whooh, hoohooh!"

Walter puckered his lips, scratched his bottom, and with his arms dangling low, he ambled off in search of trees to swing from.

Folk in the shopping district shook their heads sadly at the boy who stood shouting aloud, "I'm Henry Mawdsley, the world's worst liar!"

73

A chorus of agreement echoed back from five hundred mouths. "Yes, you are!"

"Honestly I am, the worst liar in the world!"

"We believe you, Henry Mawdsley!" they called back en masse.

The seventh day drew inevitably toward its close.

It was an hour before midnight. The wind sighed like a lost soul around the deserted streets and rain lashed ceaselessly upon the gilded plate-glass windows of the town's fanciest restaurant. Henry Mawdsley poked his fork glumly at a giant whipped cream and spun-chocolate eclair, a half-finished can of cola stood in a champagne bucket full of ice at his elbow. He moodily dismissed the headwaiter, who was standing by with a tray of lobster fricasseed in lemonade with marshmallows (one of Henry's favorite dishes whose recipe he had given to the special chef).

"Take it away, Duprez. The very thought of eating food tonight makes me feel quite ill. I can't bear the sight or the smell of it near me without wanting to be sick."

The headwaiter's face took on a distinctly greenish pallor at this remark. "My feelings also, Monsieur Henri!"

The temperamental Duprez flung the dish through the open doors, out onto the pavement. It was followed by a veritable cartload of food from the other diners, all of whom had to believe Henry and were feeling quite sickened. Some of them began actually fighting each other to phone for ambulances because Henry had mentioned sickness. Normally this would have caused Henry to roar with laughter, but a deep depression had settled over the head of Henry Mawdsley. The time was drawing near when Nick Lucifer would leave his fiery regions to claim Henry's soul. The awful realization of what would befall him when the clock struck twelve began to dawn upon him.

Then the restaurant lights went out.

"Evairyone remain calm, eef you please. I am certain it is, 'ow you say, a small electrical fault."

Duprez lit a candle on one of the tables. Other diners (some still feeling sick) followed his example.

Immediately the restaurant became a cavern of flickering yellow light and dancing shadows. The short hairs on the back of Henry's neck stood up rigid. Nick Lucifer was sitting next to him.

"Time to go, Henry Mawdsley!"

A howling gust of wind slammed both the restaurant doors wide open. All the candles were extinguished by the gale. Nick Lucifer took firm hold of Henry's arm, and, as if in a dream, Henry allowed himself to be led out into the street. A large black old-fashioned limousine with no driver was parked at the curb. At a snap of Nick Lucifer's fingers the doors creaked slowly open.

"Back to my office, boy. We have business to conclude."

The big black car slid noiselessly through the rainwashed streets and the moonless night. Henry Mawdsley stared miserably out of the darkened windows at the town he would never see again. Nick Lucifer produced a lighted cigar and a glass of port wine from his pocket. He sipped and puffed triumphantly as he surveyed his glum victim.

"Well, Henry, cat got your tongue? No more lies to tell me?"

The car came to a halt in the park, right beside the

bench where the two had first met each other. Henry felt something shove him outward. He landed upon the gravel path; the big black car had vanished. He was alone with Nick Lucifer.

"Now there's only you and me, Henry, nobody else. Still, I don't suppose anyone would believe all of this. But we know different, eh?"

Henry nodded dumbly as Nick Lucifer walked into the bushes. Crimson light and amber fumes poured forth from the underworld. "Follow me, Henry, let me show you your new home. It's just beneath my office. About four hundred miles down."

Henry felt his legs moving. He was walking toward the fiery pit when a voice like a thousand harps playing in a sunlit glade halted his progress.

"Stop, Satan, you have no right to possess this mortal soul!"

A blazing golden radiance shone about the form of the speaker. Henry blinked. Nick Lucifer covered his eyes and muttered something completely unprintable as the Archangel Gabriel approached. Henry forgot his peril momentarily—he had never seen a real angel before. Gabriel stood at least a foot and a half taller than any human (because of his large folded wings, which looked like an immense white mohican punk hairdo). He wore a soft white flowing garment and had the kindest blue eyes in the universe. His voice rang out like several hundred ghetto blasters relaying Beethoven's *Pastorale*. "Back, back to your pit of Eblis. Begone, Beelzebub, Lord of the Flies, you shall not have the soul of Henry Mawdsley!"

Nick Lucifer produced the scrolled parchment. Puffing furiously on his cigar he waved the document aloft.

"Don't try the old heavenly rescuer with me, Gabe. I've got this one's soul, signed for with his own name in his own blood, right here!"

The Archangel placed himself firmly between Henry and the Devil, a quiet smile of confidence playing about his angelic lips.

"Are you sure? Have you checked the signature?"

Nick Lucifer scowled darkly.

"Of course I'm sure. I knew this boy was a dreadful liar, so I exerted my powers and looked deep into his mind. I am certain he signed his real name to this agreement. I have no need to look. The tricks of one small boy are as nothing to the Lord of Darkness."

Gabriel gave the worried Henry a light shove toward the Devil. "Then you may take him, Evil One. But woe betide you if you try to possess a soul under false contract. Beware the wrath from above. Personally I'd look at the signature if I were you."

Nick Lucifer produced a pair of super bifocal reading glasses from the night air. Gabriel was not impressed with hellish conjuring—he had witnessed every trick in the book, and then some.

As Nick Lucifer scanned the parchment Henry felt his stomach begin to churn and his legs turn to jelly. The angel pointed a celestially manicured finger at the scrawl on the bottom line of the contract. "There, you see, signed in port wine; the boy never used blood."

Satan glared foully at Henry as his mind raced back to the signing of the scroll. The billowing cloud of sulphur smoke, the wretched boy not wanting either of them to see him pierce his finger. Of course, the devious little worm had dipped the pen in port wine, it had been there on the table by him. Nick Lucifer sought all his Satanic powers of contractual understanding and suddenly he laughed triumphantly. It took the Devil to find the right loophole.

"Haha! But nevertheless, I have his signature here. Signed in blood, lemonade, tomato ketchup, or port wine, it doesn't really matter as long as it's the right signature."

Gabriel tittered, very undignified for an angel.

"And *is* that the right signature?"

Nick Lucifer looked puzzled.

"Well, of course it is! Maybe it's very scrawly, but lots of my clients had squiggly signatures: Attila the Hun, Adolf Hitler, Blackbeard the Pirate. I've had famous doctors whose signatures you wouldn't recognize, eminent lawyers, top politicians. What's all the fuss over one silly schoolboy's signature?"

Gabriel could not resist a heavenly smirk.

"All of their signatures could be compared against records and found to be true, badly written or not. But none of them were like Henry Mawdsley."

"What?"

The archangel produced a celestial golden retractable pen and a junior cherub's exercise book from under his wing. (He was also very good at conjuring in a heavenly fashion.)

"Henry, I'd like you to sign your name on the front of this book."

Henry took the pen. He screwed up his eyes, his tongue stuck out one corner of his mouth, and he laboriously tried to do as he was bidden.

Gabriel held up the result for Satan's inspection.

"See, it comes out different every time. Henry Mawdsley can neither read, spell, nor write. Read your own contract, paragraph B clause six, which states: 'Whereby any mortal signing this contract must have complete knowledge of what he (the victim) is signing his name or affixing a recognized signature to. Furthermore, said victim must be deemed able to read in full the contract and scribe a genuine signature or make his mark, usually in the form of an X, or any other mark familiar as his personal monogram to all and sundry.' Tut tut, it appears you've been fooled by a schoolboy."

Smoke belched from Nick Lucifer's eyeballs and ears. He drummed his hooves against the ground. Grabbing Henry he thrust a pen (also produced out of midair) into the boy's grubby hand.

"Here, sign an X on the bottom of this form."

With a look of fierce concentration Henry scrawled a backward Z.

Nick Lucifer tore a large chunk from his tail in fury.

Henry tried again, this time it was an upside down T.

Satan grabbed the pen and wrote with bold strokes at the foot of the scroll.

"Look! This is an X, and here's another, quite simple, here's another. Just two diagonal strokes crossing each other, can't you even do that?"

Henry looked at the Archangel Gabriel.

"He's beginning to sound like my teacher, Mrs. Benson. She says I'd try the patience of a saint; she never mentioned the Devil, though."

Gabriel shook his head. A pinion feather stuck in his eye and he dabbed at it with a beautifully laundered handkerchief.

Nick Lucifer's horns drooped. "But where does all this leave me?"

Gabriel put a protective arm around Henry. "Well where d'you suppose it leaves you, without a client and you can think yourself lucky you didn't get this boy under false pretenses. It could have led to a shutdown on your burners for a year. Oh, just a moment."

The angel extended his arms and clicked his fingers. The contract disappeared in a puff of extra-white smoke.

"That'll save you putting it through your hellish parchment shredder. Now be off with you. I'm sure you've got lots of evil things to do down there without hanging around parks, wilting the grass all night."

Henry waved as he went off hand in hand with the mighty archangel. "Goodbye, Mr. Lucifer. P'raps you would have been better off taking those Australian pesetas my dad sent me."

"Yaaaaaggggghhhhh!"

Nick Lucifer stuffed his tail in his mouth, bit down hard on it and vanished in a cloud of purplish-green smoke.

Henry Mawdsley bid farewell to his friend and rescuer at the park gates. "Goodbye, Mr. Gabriel, and thanks for all you've done for me. If you're ever in the neighborhood again why not drop into our house? My mom makes great angel cake, she's always doing that when angels call to see us." He jotted something down and handed it to Gabriel.

There was his name and address perfectly written.

As he watched the small figure skip off down the road, the Archangel Gabriel shook his head and smiled.

"Well, I knew Henry Mawdsley would lie to the very Devil himself, but fancy fooling Mrs. Benson and me!"

5

No doubt you've heard of Neptune,
and of the mermaids too;
or the legend of the Lorelei,
and the fabled naiads who
inhabit the world 'neath the waters.
They don't need to come up for air,
these spirits of the oceans and deeps,
with wavy trailing hair.
But far from the sea and its spirits
in a woodland lake or pond,
you may spy a piece of waterweed,
a harmless waving frond.
Stranger, beware, for the Grimblett lives there.
What is it? Nobody knows.
Just something time has forgotten
that lies underwater and grows.
Bad fortune to unbelievers
who think it's just waterweed.
For Grimbletts were ever deceivers,
and very revengeful indeed. . . .

Bridgey

"Sure and aren't ducks the greatest things in all the world!" Bridgey spoke her thoughts aloud to the white mists as they curled in wraithlike tendrils across the surface of the morning lake. The ducks ignored her completely, quacking and yammering the day's business among themselves as they waddled and trundled fussily into the water, led by Rafferty, the leader of the drakes.

Bridgey wiggled the toes of her bare feet in the mud at the water's edge as she talked to them. The ducks were used to the sound of the little girl's voice. "Now don't stray too close by those bushes on the other side. Who knows, some divvil of a fox or ferret might devour you, feathers and all."

Rafferty began paddling over to the very spot Bridgey had warned them about. She stamped her foot, causing mud to splatter the frayed hem of her skirt, and waving a willow twig at the drake, she called out, "Mister Rafferty, are you deaf or just disobedient? What've I told you? Get out of there this very instant!"

Rafferty did a stately turn, cruising out into the center of the lake, with an ill-assorted two dozen followers in his wake. Bridgey was still shaking the stick in reprimand.

"And stay away from there, d'ye hear me, or I'll tickle your tail with this stick, so I will. Wipe that silly smile off your beak, Mister Rafferty, and that goes for the rest of you. Stay this side, where I can see you well. The lake's safe, sure there's only the ould Grimblett down there—he watches over little maids and disobedient ducks good enough, 'tis his job."

"Bridgey!"

She flinched momentarily at the sound of her uncle's voice.

"I'm over here by the lake, Uncle Sully."

Sully McConville trod gingerly through the mud to his small niece.

"Have y'cleaned the duckpens out, girl?"

"I have so, while you were still abed."

"Less of your lip. How many eggs today?"

"Seven and twenty, Uncle."

Bridgey smelled the raw whiskey on her uncle's breath as he brought his unshaven face close to her. McConville's bleary red-veined eyes shifted slyly as he grabbed the willow twig from Bridgey's hand.

"Are y'telling me the truth now?"

"I am so, Uncle Sully."

He twitched the stick close to her nose.

"If you're lyin' I'll skelp the skin off your bones, girl. I think you're going soft in the head, talking to yourself out here. What's all this about a Grimblett?"

Bridgey remained silent in the face of her uncle's sour temper. Sully growled at the mud which had seeped in through his leaky boot soles.

"Go on up to the house now. Put the kettle on for tea and boil me two eggs in it, no, make that three. I'll be taking the other two dozen in to sell at Ballymain market. Cut me three slices of white bread and put the honey jar on the table. Move yourself now!"

He snapped the twig and hurled it out into the lake, causing the ducks to quack and swim off in a half flutter. Digging a broken yellowed clay pipe out of his vest pocket Sully sucked on it. He spat noisily into the lake, calling after the girl, "And you know what you'll get if I catch you eatin' eggs, honey or white bread, me lady."

Bridgey called back cheerfully, "Aye, so I do. You'll skelp the skin off me bones!"

She busied herself around the ill-equipped kitchen of the crumbling cottage, murmuring to herself happily. "Oho, Sully McConville, don't you think yourself the big bold man now. But you'll find that you can't throw broken sticks or spit into the Grimblett's lake without the creature himself knowing it. Sure, wasn't I a witness to the whole thing meself, to say nothing of Mister Rafferty and his ducks. Small wonder they were all smilin' to themselves. Finer men than yourself haven't got away with less."

The kettle was bubbling merrily as Bridgey spooned three duck eggs into the water. Facing the open window, she laid the well-scrubbed wooden table with white bread and a brownstone crock jar of honey for her greedy uncle. There was buttermilk and two of last night's cold boiled potatoes, still in their skins, for Bridgey's breakfast. She watched Sully walk up from the lake, shaking mud from his boots and muttering darkly to himself about the injustices of life. The mist had begun to disperse under a yellow late spring sun, and Bridgey could make out the Grimblett. It was lying just beneath the clear surface of the lake, all green and misty, spreading wavery tentacles far and wide across its realm.

"You look fit and well today, Grimblett, though I can tell you're angry with me uncle Sully, and sure, why wouldn't you be? The way he sucks that dirty pipe and spits on you every day. I'll have to go now; he's coming for his breakfast. I'll talk to you later."

Sully McConville sat across the table from his niece, watching her as he sucked tea noisily from a chipped mug. Bridgey kept her eyes down, munching industriously on the potatoes and washing them down with sips of buttermilk. Sully wiped his mouth on the back of his sleeve.

"Eat up now, girl, and thank the Lord who left me to

84

provide for you after your ma and da passed on. Leave a clean plate now, and thank God for his goodness and bounty."

He cracked an egg and spooned it hastily into his mouth, yellow runny yolk dribbling through the coarse whiskers onto his chin. Tearing a crust from the bread he dipped it in the honey and sucked noisily on it. Bridgey could not help the disgust that showed on her face. Sully wagged the crust at her across the table.

"Straighten your gob, girl, or I'll skelp the skin off your bones. Duck eggs are too rich for children and the honey would only bring you out in a rash of pimples. I need it for me chest." Here he coughed to illustrate the point. "Taters and buttermilk are what I was brought up on. They never harmed me, so you eat up now."

"I will, Uncle."

"And don't waste any. There's goodness in potato skins."

"I'm not wasting any at all, Uncle."

"Well make sure you don't."

Bridgey would rather have died than eat a duck egg. The ducks were her friends and she had seen the ducklings that came from the eggs, little, downy, smiling creatures, with tiny comical wings. But white bread and honey, that was a different matter altogether. She had dipped soft white bread into the honey when her uncle was absent—it tasted like heaven on earth. Then one day Sully had caught her; he had beaten her soundly with a blackthorn stick he kept behind the door. Bridgey had never stolen bread and honey again, though she often dreamed of the bread, with its fresh smell and crispy crust, together with the sweet, heavy, mysterious stickiness of deep amber honey, with chewy fragments of combwax which clung to the teeth. Sully's voice broke in on her imaginings.

85

"Right, I'm off now to the Ballymain market. Mind you boil those taters the way I like them, so they're floury when they split. See to the ducks, put fresh straw in their pens, and tidy up around here. Sweep the floor, wash the dishes, and scrub the table well. I'll be back at nightfall, and you know what'll happen to you if there's anything amiss, Bridgey."

"You'll skelp the skin off me bones, Uncle."

"Aye, so I will."

Sully licked honey from his whiskers, belched, lighted his pipe and set his hat on squarely. Then he left for Ballymain market.

The afternoon was peaceful; under the warm sun the lake lay smooth and placid. Even the ducks had stopped paddling; they floated about silently, napping in the noontide. Mister Rafferty stood on the bank, gently squelching the mud under his webbed feet. Though he was facing away from the house his bright little eye oscillated backwards, as he watched Bridgey come to the water's edge, her bare feet disturbing the thin crust that the sun had baked upon the mud. Rafferty gave a short quack of welcome, declining to comment further on the loaf and honey crock which the little girl placed upon a stone. She sat down next to them. The drake wandered over, his slim graceful neck nodding slightly as he waddled. Bridgey passed her hand gently over his sleek head.

"Good afternoon to you, sir. Have you had enough of the swimming?"

Mister Rafferty nodded and settled down by her.

"Ah well, your family look all nice and peaceful there. See Matilda with her head beneath her wing, fast asleep, Lord love her."

Drake and girl sat watching the water. Bridgey half closed her eyes and began intoning in a soft singsong voice.

"Grimblett, Grimblett, are you there?"

The lake stayed calm and unruffled.

"I know for sure you're out there, Grimblett. Will y'not bid me a good afternoon?"

Out upon the middle of the waters a single large bubble plopped and gurgled, causing ripples to widen across the surface. Bridgey and Mister Rafferty nodded knowingly.

"Ah, you're still angered over Sully spittin' and throwing sticks at you this morning."

Once more the lake bubbled and gurgled. This time a frond of the heavy green weed that lay beneath the surface rose momentarily clear of the waters; then it slid back under. Bridgey sighed. "Well I'm sorry for you, but there's little Rafferty or I can do."

A huge bubble, like an upturned bathtub, gurgled its way into the noon air; more ripples began, stretching in circles until small waves lapped over Bridgey's toes. She stood up.

"I'll tell you what I'll do, Grimblett. I'll pour a bit of this honey to you, some bread and all. That should make you feel better, eh?"

This time the lake lay still.

Bridgey broke the bread and scattered it on the water. Immediately the ducks came awake and swam over to gobble it up, though Mister Rafferty remained faithfully at her side. Bridgey picked up the honey crock.

"Oh come on now, Grimblett, don't be sulking on such a fine afternoon. See, you were too late to get the bread, now Mister Rafferty's family've eaten it. Here, try some honey. You'll like it, the taste is like flowers and meadows in summer. Come on now."

Bridgey tilted the crock, shaking it vigorously to make the honey flow. Rafferty watched her intently. The honey did not seem too keen on leaving its container, though a very small amount oozed out onto

87

Bridgey's fingers. She licked the stickiness and rinsed her hands in the lake, cajoling her friend the Grimblett.

"Ah c'mon now, don't be shy. You'll enjoy it."

Upending the crock, she shook it hard. The smooth glazed earthenware jar shot from between her wet hands and rolled away underwater down the steep lake bed before Bridgey could do anything about it. She slumped on the stone, holding her hands across her eyes, trying not to believe what she had just done.

"Heaven preserve me. Uncle Sully will skelp the skin off me bones with his blackthorn stick. I know he will, he'll have me very life! Grimblett, is there nothing you can do to save a little maid. Roll the crock back to me. Oh please!"

The water bubbled apologetically and lay calm. Mister Rafferty placed his bill sympathetically in Bridgey's lap as his family paddled close in and floated there, watching her. Slow minutes of the sunny noontide ebbed inexorably away. Bridgey's tears flowed along with them.

Nothing could hold back time and the return of Sully McConville from Ballymain market. Bridgey had cried herself to sleep by the lake; she awakened with the slight chill of advancing eventide to a reddening sky in which the sun sank gloriously, like a peach dipped into port wine. Hurrying to the house Bridgey rushed about like a dervish, setting the pot of potatoes on its tripod over the fire and tossing in a dash of salt. As if to redeem her quivering flesh from the crime she had committed the little girl set about her chores with furious energy, piling turf on the fire, scrubbing the table, sweeping the hard packed earth floor with a broom until dust flew widespread, wiping that same dust from shelf, table, chair and windows with a cheesecloth. She put just the right amount of leaves into the battered teapot and trimmed the lamp wick to even the flame as darkness fell. Inside, the cottage was as fresh as new paint. Bridgey stood at the open door, her heart beating fitfully against the leaden weight within her chest as she watched her uncle Sully staggering up the path through the darkness.

It was evident that he had been drinking by the way he weaved to and fro. Under his arm Sully carried a bottle and a piece of smoke-cured bacon from Ballymain market, to supplement his supper of boiled potatoes. He brushed past Bridgey and sat heavily in his chair, slamming down the bacon upon the table.

"Bridgey, slice some of this up an' fry it for me, a man needs some meat now and again. It's no good for children, mind, too fat an' salty. Well, don't stand there gawpin' with cow's eyes, move yourself, girl, or it'll be mornin' soon."

With trembling hands she cut the bacon into rough slices, setting it on the frying pan to sizzle as she drained off the water from the potatoes . . . fearful that any moment her uncle might call for bread and honey. Sully, however, was not looking to satisfy his sweet tooth, not while there was whiskey to be had. Weary and footsore after the long trek home from Ballymain, he kicked off his boots and pulled the chair up to the fire. Lighting his clay pipe with a spill he started drinking straight from the bottle. Bridgey worked with quick, nervous energy, laying out his plate of food at the table and pouring a mug of tea for him. She gave a fearful start at the sound of Sully's voice.

"Is that the ducks I can hear still out on the lake, girl?"

"Ducks? Oh I must have forgotten. I'll get them into the pen right away. Come and have your supper, Uncle

89

Sully. It's on the table, all nice and hot."

He swigged at the bottle. His pipe lay forgotten on the hearth.

"I'll Uncle Sully you, idle little brat. Never mind the supper. You get those ducks in or I'll skelp the skin off your bones!"

Bridgey fled the cottage, hurrying through the night to the water's edge. Mister Rafferty stood on the bank. Cocking his head on one side he quacked wearily. Bridgey could make out the shapes of other ducks, asleep on the far bank.

"Oh Mister Rafferty, there you are. I'm sorry I forgot to take you and your family to the pens. You've not been fed either. 'Tis all me own fault, I'm a terrible girl."

The drake stretched himself, spreading his wings he quacked aloud his various complaints. Bridgey cast an uneasy glance at the cottage. "Hush now, or you'll have me uncle out here with his great stick. Listen, we'll never get those others off the far bank until morning. You bide here and hold your noise; I've got to go back to the house. I promise you'll come to no harm. The Grimblett will watch over you and your family, I know he will."

Mister Rafferty settled his neck down on his crop feathers as Bridgey ran off into the darkness. Behind him the surface of the lake threw up a few bubbles before subsiding into the calm of a late spring night.

Bridgey breathed a small sob of relief; Uncle Sully had fallen asleep in his chair by the fire. Carefully she removed the quarter-full whiskey bottle from between his limp fingers and set it on the table, alongside the now cold bacon and potatoes. It was not unusual for him to sleep all night in front of the fire, fully dressed, after he had been drinking. Safe for the night at least, Bridgey backed up the fire with damp slow-burning turf. Taking some potatoes in a clean piece of cloth she went back to the lake with an old shawl wrapped about her shoulders. Sully McConville snored gently, his mouth half open, chin on chest and hands lying loosely upon his stomach as it heaved up and down in the flickering shadows of the warm room.

Out by the lake Bridgey perched on a stone, sharing her meal of cold cooked potato with Mister Rafferty. A thin moon sliver hung over the lake like a slice of lemon rind, turning the water to a light golden shimmer, backed by the silhouette of the trees which massed on the far lakeshore. Bridgey murmured softly to her friend, "There's a fear in me for what the morn will bring. I wish it could stay peaceful night forever, so I do."

Beside her the drake blinked his bright little eyes and smiled that secret smile that only ducks and drakes know the meaning of.

Sully groaned aloud as morning sunlight cascaded through the windowpanes to set his brain afire. Flaming orange motes danced a jig before his half opened eyes; sour whiskey taste clogged his furred tongue as his temples thrummed with the father of all headaches. In a petulant croak he called out, "Bridgey, bring the honey, girl!"

There was no answer. Sully heaved himself painfully out of his chair. The embers of the fire were hidden beneath thick grey ash. With ill-tempered bile rising within him he glared at the cold teapot beside the cold bacon and potatoes on the table. Tripping over his boots he cursed and kicked at them.

"Bridgey, bring me the honey an' a spoon, or I'll skelp the skin off your bones. Bridgey, where are y'girl?"

Stumbling and muttering he searched shelf and cupboard for the crock, longing for the soothing sweetness of honey to drive away the whiskey bitterness from his mouth. The quacking of unfed ducks down at the lake diverted his attention. He fumbled with the latch and swung the door ajar, wincing at the stream of sunlight which shafted in like a volley of golden arrows.

There she was, the idle little brat, curled up on a stone with a shawl around her and that cheeky old drake. This time he would teach her a lesson that she'd remember to her dying day!

Snatching the blackthorn stick from behind the door he roared like a wounded lion.

"Bridgeeeeeeee!"

Like a shot the little girl sprang up. Mister Rafferty, quacking and ruffled, slid from her knees awkwardly. Bridgey's face went white with fright at the sight of her uncle brandishing the blackthorn stick as he strode barefoot toward her.

"Er, er, top of the mornin' to you, sir. I was about to feed the ducks."

A large vein stood out on Sully's temple, pulsing like a nightingale's throat. His voice was thick and harsh.

"Feed the ducks, is it? What about me, don't I get fed? The place is like a midden—cold food, no fire, no tea or honey, and you out here sleepin' your shiftless life away!"

Sully had begun moving this way and that, cutting off any possible retreat. Bridgey had the lake at her back. There was no way she might avoid a skelping.

"Uncle, I'm sorry, it wasn't my fault. Me hands were wet an' the honey crock slipped off into the water. I'll never do it again."

Sully smiled wickedly, raising the heavy stick.

92

"So, you'll not do it again, eh girl. You'll be lucky if you have legs to stand on after I'm done with you, me lazy scut!"

He swung the stick in a vicious arc. Bridgey dodged to one side. Sully slipped and fell heavily in the mud; he came up shouting and covered in brown slime.

"Cummere, I'll skelp the skin off your bo—"

And then Mister Rafferty was upon him, quacking and flapping. As if on a given signal the ducks came out with a rush from the water and piled in on Sully. Bridgey could hardly make out her uncle—he was enveloped in hissing, quacking, feather-beating, web-clawing birds. Sully lost the blackthorn stick in the mud. Frantically he beat about, his arms milling wide, slipping, falling, skidding in the slutchy mud as he ranted and roared.

"I'll kill yeh, d'you hear me! I'll wring your blasted necks!"

Out in the middle of the lake bubbles began bursting on the surface. Bridgey cried aloud in terror.

"Save us, Grimblett! Oh do something, please!"

Sully thrust the birds from him with a mighty effort and stepped backward to gain a breathing space.

But he stepped back into the lake!

He slid in the sloping shallows and overbalanced. Blowing water from his nostrils and wiping his face upon a wet sleeve he stood there, his clawing hands shaking at Bridgey.

"I'll throttle the life from yeh, you and those ducks!"

The lake behind Sully McConville began bubbling madly, as if the waters were boiling. He tried pulling himself forward but slid further backwards. Something was wrapped around his feet; he felt the water lapping about his chest. A look of fear crossed his ugly features.

"Bridgey, help me, girl. Help me!"

Now the thick, trailing green fronds appeared. They draped about his arms and neck, caressing him with coldness they had fetched up from the depths. Sully tried feebly to fight against them, but they piled upon him like the tentacles of some unknown emerald monster. Colossal bubbles created waves upon the lake that filled his mouth and flooded his ears.

"Save me, girl, Bridgeeeeeee!"

She watched, fascinated, as a waving sloppy frond wrapped itself around her uncle's mouth and nostrils, stifling his cries forever. Back, back he was dragged until he vanished beneath the surface. The waters gave one final bulking swirl; a single bubble burst up from the depths into the sunlight. Then calm reigned over the scene. To any passing traveller it would have made a charming rustic picture: the little ragged girl standing in the sunshine with her ducks on the banks of a quiet lake.

Sully McConville's boots burned merrily on the turf fire. Bridgey sat in his chair, Mister Rafferty at her feet like a faithful pet dog. Ducks perched on the shelf, windowsill and table, some of them eating the remains of the cold potatoes from the supper plate. Bridgey stirred the drake gently with her bare foot.

"Mister Rafferty, d'you think you could tell your family to lay lots of eggs? Then in a day or two perhaps you and me will go to Ballymain market and get more honey, white bread too. You'd like that, wouldn't you? Sure it's grand stuff the honey is."

She rose and went to lean on the windowsill, gazing out at the lake. "And yourself, Grimblett, we'll bring honey back for you and all. Sure, it'll help you to get rid of the nasty taste, so it will."

6

Waiting, waiting, year by year,
as centuries turn to dust;
here's a ghost you shouldn't fear,
whose tale is so unjust.
Waiting through each season
in a wayside lane,
for a simple reason—
loneliness and pain.
Will you see him as you pass,
Gilly, standing there
midst the hedges and the grass?
His life was so unfair.
Waiting, waiting, year by year,
till winter has begun,
or when the spring is drawing near,
through rain and wind and sun.
Far away the birds may fly,
'cross clouds, 'neath skies of grey—
hear the ghostly boy's sad cry.
Oh why must Gilly stay?

The Sad History of Gilly Bodkin

Life had never been much fun for Gilly Bodkin.

Death was even less of a joke, considering that he had been confined to the same field and lane since the day of his untimely end. That event had taken place in the year 1690, though Gilly was not much good at dates and figures, or reading and writing—in fact he was a total stranger to anything remotely connected to learning. Being the son of a peasant laborer and one of a family of thirteen children, the chances of his being educated were extremely thin, so any scrap of knowledge Gilly had acquired was from his parents or kin. He knew that one cow made one, two cows were a pair, and beyond that it was either a "big herd," or a "mizzuble little 'un." Chickens, pigs, horses and goats were much the same, so were people. Gilly recalled having his ears soundly boxed by his mother for calling Squire Manfield's four daughters a mizzuble little herd.

"They un's ain't no herd, them be a family," his mother had said. This was a bit too much for Gilly to take in. Besides, the four Manfield girls were indeed a mizzuble little herd to him, and that was that! Gilly did not like them anyway, living up at that great fancy house, dressing up like prize horses for fairtime, all those ribbons and folderols. They rode about in a painted coach, forever stuffing their greedy mouths with candies and sweetmeats. Like his brothers and sisters, Gilly went barefoot in all weathers, dressed in cast-off rags and sacking. As for food, Gilly's family ate much the same as the Squire's animals: turnips, cabbage, carrots, whatever happened to be growing from the ground at the time.

96

Gilly had watched the Manfield girls eating sugar sticks and other confections. They slurped, licked, fought and crunched like four young porkers let loose in the orchard to eat windfall apples and pears. Gilly longed to taste sweetmeats, almond fingers, fruit truffles, toffee apples, vanilla pastilles, candied dates, and above all, sugar sticks. He imagined they would taste sweeter than the apple he had once stolen from Squire's orchard. His father had caught him and belted him black and blue for thieving from their benefactor, punctuating each word with a slap as he lectured his son on the error of his ways.

"Apples is for gentlefolk, 'cepting those as falls to the ground. They's for pigs and 'orses, not for the likes of you. Them apples be so sweet they're like to drive us 'n's mad, Squire says. He'd be well within his rights to 'ang you, Gilly, a thievin' from his fine orchard like that."

However, it did not alter Gilly Bodkin's resolution, if sweetmeats were sweeter than apples then he must taste one for himself.

It was coming up to Michaelmas. Squire Manfield was due to take his wife, children and body servants to the town. The only one of the Bodkin family who had ever been to a town was Gilly's father, and he had never fully recovered from the shock.

"On my oath, town be full of folk! Great herds of 'em, and 'ouses too, some builded one against t'other, like so many 'orses teamed up in line. Even the floors be covered with stones. The coaches made such a clatter and a din, I thought I'd lose my senses with all the great noise!"

Giles Bodkin was an honest man, not given to

untruths. The family marveled at the idea of such a place, as they sat around the fire on the earth floor of their meager hovel. Who would have thought it, all those houses and coaches and horses and stone floors too!

From the side of the path Gilly watched Squire Manfield's coach draw near as it began the annual journey to town. Though he was greatly feared of horses, the lad stood his ground. With a creaking and rumbling of woodwork and harness the swaying carriage jolted its way along the uneven path, the driver whistling and snapping the reins along the coach-horses' broad backs. Squire Manfield followed behind, jogging grandly along on his huge white stallion. Inside the coach Lady Manfield and two maidservants sat facing the four little girls. She sighed regretfully: Manfield would have given half his estate for a son and heir. The four girls fought and argued petulantly as they ravaged the contents of a basket full of sweetmeats.

"Mamma, Mamma, Agnes has taken my sugar stick!"

"Liar! I did not. You've already had one."

"Leave that toffee apple alone. It's mine, Lucy!"

"Greedy greedy pig. Fattie!"

"Ooh, Mamma, did you hear that? Jessie called me fattie!"

Gilly ran alongside the coach, jumping up and down to catch sight of Squire's mizzuble little herd, gorging on sweetmeats. He caught glimpses of them, their fat little faces never still, munching, crunching and sucking furiously, each worrying that the other might get more than her share. What made him do it Gilly never knew, but he suddenly found himself shouting to them.

"Hoi there, missies, I be Gilly Bodkin. I ain't never

98

tasted sweetmeats. Do you feel free to toss some out to me?"

Agnes stared from the coach window, her piggy eyes agape at the insolent boy shouting at them.

"If I owned sweetmeats I'd give some to thee," the boy went on. "Go on, throw some to Gilly. You uns got a basket of 'em in there."

Agnes took the sugar stick from her mouth only long enough to spit at the cheeky ragamuffin. Gilly ducked, though he had no need to. The wind drove the sticky saliva back into Agnes's face; it dribbled over her chin as she stuck the sugar stick firmly back into her mouth. Lady Manfield grimaced with distaste as she addressed her maidservant. "Bessy, wipe Agnes's chin and tell that silly boy to go away."

The young maidservant plucked the sugar stick from Agnes's mouth. She set about wiping the child's chin on the corner of her apron. Still holding the sugar stick gingerly she enquired of her mistress, "What am I to do with this, Marm?"

Lady Manfield sniffed. "Throw it away. She's had quite enough."

"Waaah, I want my sugar stick, Mamma!"

"I said throw it away, Bessy, this instant!"

The sugar stick sailed out of the coach window into the air. Still pelting barefoot alongside the coach, Gilly could not believe his luck. They were actually throwing him sweetmeats from the coach. He leapt high, yelling with delight, trying to catch the sugar stick before it hit the muddy path as the coach rolled by. Squire Manfield's stallion was skittish; it shied up on its hind legs, throwing the Squire from his saddle. The horse's steel-shod hooves came down fast and hard, right on the skull of Gilly Bodkin. The last thing he saw before the stallion's hooves snuffed his life out was the sugar stick, as it landed upright in the mud like a small javelin. Gilly's hand reached out for it as he died.

The coach driver and the manservant sitting beside him leaped down from their seats, to assist the Squire as the coach ground to a halt. Gilly's father came running over from the fields, a billhook in one hand, a half cut turnip in the other, fearful of the Squire's wrath. In high bad temper Squire Manfield allowed the two men to assist him to his feet. He shoved them angrily from him, waving his riding crop at Giles Bodkin.

"Devil take the silly little rip! Leaping and yelling like that in front of me stallion. What was it all about?"

Giles touched a grimy but respectful finger to his forehead.

"I'm afeared I don't know. Be you 'urted, Squire, Sir?"

"No, Bodkin, though me velveteen coat's covered in mud, look at it. I think me stallion knocked a bit of sense into that brat of yours though. That'll teach him a lesson he won't forget, eh."

The coach driver stirred Gilly's limp form with his boot. "The life's gone from him, Squire. Lookit that great welt alongside his temple, Sir. He be dead as a post, I'm certain."

Stiffly the Squire remounted. He sat looking at the dead Gilly as his stallion picked up the discarded sugar stick in its huge teeth and swallowed it in a single crunch.

"Hmm, it was the boy's own stupid fault, Bodkin."

Giles rubbed his hands together nervously.

"O that it were, Squire Sir. Now don't you worry your 'ead none over Gilly, he be gone an' that be that.

We still got a great many mouths left t'feed beside missus an' me. T'weren't your fault, Sir."

Squire Manfield wiped mud from his waistcoat. "Hmph! I should say it wasn't. Y'can count yourself lucky I wasn't injured; the fall would've killed a lesser man. I'll have to get me good riding coat and britches cleaned specially when we reach town. You can do a week's work at the stables, that should cover the cost."

Giles Bodkin bowed respectfully. "Yes, Sir, thankee, Sir."

Lady Manfield was irritated at the delay.

"Rupert, what *is* going on back there? We'll never get to town at this rate."

Manfield ordered his driver and servant back to the coach. "Coming m'dear." He pointed at the body of Gilly with his crop. "I trust you'll tidy this off the path right away, eh."

The coach rumbled off down the path. Agnes got her own way as usual; she was allowed another sugar stick to keep her quiet.

Giles Bodkin looked after the departing coach and spat on the earth. "Blast all the gentry, an' damnation to yeh, Squire. Treats your beasts better than your workers. Killin' a child o' mine an a worryin' more about your precious coat 'n' britches. Aye but that's your right, ain't it? The power of life an' death o'er the likes of us."

Gilly was buried with scant ceremony. Wrapped in sacking he was bundled doubled up in a deep hole his father and brothers had dug by the side of the path, close by where he had died. Several of the young Bodkins stood watching as it was filled in. Afterward they helped their father roll a huge boulder on the grave to mark the spot. Gilly's mother sniffed as she wiped her eyes on a tattered shawl.

"He were always a-gettin' daft notions, mad he were for ought that was sweet. Lack a day, what's done can't be undone. We'd best be about our work, t'wont get done by itself."

Shooing the little ones before them like so many chickens, Giles Bodkin and his wife went back to chopping turnips for the Squire's livestock, and themselves. The grave stood forlorn at the pathside.

A moonless rainswept night had descended over ditch, field and hedgerow. The wind keened mournfully, scouring the wintry countryside, singing a bleak dirge of colder days to come.

Gilly's head ached.

He sat on the boulder at the side of the path feeling very puzzled.

What was he doing outside on a night like this? Normally he would have been huddled around the fire with his family. The mystery intensified when he realized that in spite of the rain, he was neither cold nor wet, though his head ached painfully.

Slowly he rose and started making his way homeward. His mother and father would scold him when he got back, calling him silly for being out in such weather. Pushing through the gap in the hawthorn hedge Gilly tramped across the turnip field. At first he put his slow progress down to the fact that it was always difficult crossing ploughed soil when it was raining. However, he was surprised to see that his feet were not at all muddy or bogged down with soil—it was as if he could not feel the earth beneath him. He tried hurrying, but to no avail; something was drawing him back to the path. Resolutely he pressed onward, doing his best to resist the unseen force. With agonizing slowness he drew near to the low, miserable building that was his home, finally arriving at the churned-up mud in front of the door.

Try as he might Gilly could not go any further.

He heard the voices of his family inside and called out to them, "Father, Mother, Effie, Perce! Can 'ee hear me, 'tis Gilly all left 'ere alone in rain."

There was no reply. He made his way around to the single window on the south side. It lacked panes, but was loosely shuttered against the weather. Gilly could peer through the cracks and knotholes of the warped woodwork. They were crouched around a smoking fire in the center of the single low-beamed room, eating cooked turnips and supping a broth made from winter greens. He tried once again to attract their attention.

"Be you all gone deaf? 'Tis Gilly, take me in for pity's sakes!"

His sister Effie dropped her bowl and screamed with fright. "Yeeek! Mother, did 'ee 'ear that? 'Twas our Gilly a-callin' out!"

Giles Bodkin promptly cuffed her on the ear.

"'Old thy tongue, girl, 'twas only the rain an' wind outside. Silly young mare, a-wastin' good broth like that. You lay down on yonder straw an' get 'ee to sleep afore I take my belt to thee."

Outside in the mud and rain Gilly stood shaking his head wearily. It was raining and yet he was dry; it was muddy and yet he was clean; he was standing outside his own home and yet he could not enter. He tenderly touched his aching head and began drifting slowly back across the fields.

*

For some reason Gilly felt a little better sitting on his boulder at the side of the path. His head ached less and his thoughts became clearer. He began talking aloud to himself.

"Ah, 'tis sad an' lonely for a pore boy sat 'ere alone. Though I think I could manage to eat one o' those sugar sticks. They must taste sweeter'n an apple."

Muttering away, he began searching through the wet grass and sludgy puddles.

"Mayhaps Squire's 'orse didn't eat it all. Likely he left a morsel for pore Gilly."

After a while he gave up and went back to sit on his boulder. "So be it, I'll bide my time an' sit here to await the coach a-comin' back from town. Squire's stallion 'urted my skull last time it passed this way, so they'll be sure to take pity an' give me a sugar stick from that basket, just one."

It was more than a month later when Squire Manfield and his family returned from their visit to the town. Gilly saw the coach coming from afar. He stood eagerly awaiting until it drew near, then leaping up he ran alongside, shouting despite his headache.

"Kind missies, throw me a sugar stick, 'tis I, Gilly Bodkin!"

The Squire's white stallion reared up and threw him again. Once more he was unhurt but caked with mud. Inside the coach his daughter Agnes gave vent to a fat little squeal.

"Yeek! It's that nasty boy again. He wants a sugar stick, Mamma."

Lady Manfield was a picture of dignified fury, pursing her lips and waggling a finger at her daughter.

"Agnes! Hold your tongue, miss, you've made

104

yourself sick from gobbling too many sweetmeats. Sugar sticks indeed! I'll have Bessy give you a good physicking with brimstone when we get home." She leaned out the coach window and began berating her husband. "Rupert, look at your best velveteens! I told you not to drink two bottles of Malmsey at breakfast, but you know best, don't you!"

Gilly was still prancing about like a march hare, pleading aloud, "What be the matter with 'ee all, you uns gone daft? Can't 'ee see Gilly? Throw me my sugar stick an' I'll leave 'ee in peace."

Agnes buried her head in Bessy's apron and sobbed hysterically. Squire Manfield tethered his stallion to the back of the coach and climbed inside after throwing his ruined coat to the driver. "I'm bound to sell that stallion at the next fair, too skittish; that's the second time he's unseated me. It had nought to do with Malmsey, m'dear. Drive on up there, before I catch me death sittin' here in me shirt, and, Agnes, stop whinin', gel, stoppit!"

Gilly knew he was not able to pick up mud to sling after the coach; he slumped moodily on his boulder grizzling to himself. "Rotten ol' Squire an' his mizzuble little herd."

The Manfields never used the path again. The Squire gave orders to use another way that separated his route from Gilly's grave by two fields and a wooded copse. The Bodkin family grew up and left, one by one, to seek a better life in other places. Effie was the last to go, taking her aged parents with her. They went without even a backward glance at the long forgotten resting place of Gilly. As it does with all things, time took its toll of the Manfield family's fortune and lands. The Squire, being without a son, took heavily to drink; his wife died scolding him. The four daughters had married well long before this event, and moved to other parts. Manfield died alone and impoverished, overburdened by ruinous land taxes and unpaid tithes. Manfield Hall fell into disrepair as nature reclaimed the entire area, buildings, fields and lands. Gilly Bodkin still sat on his boulder by the side of the overgrown path, fervently hoping that one day a carriage containing little girls and sweetmeats would pass his way. He talked a lot to himself and nursed his headache. And waited.

It was the year 1990. Exactly three centuries had passed since Gilly's untimely end, yet the ragged boy still waited. Over the years he had caught glimpses of strange new things in the lonely rural backwater. The path was now a gravelled walk provided by the National Heritage Trust: it had been designated as part of a Nature and History walk, though few people bothered to use it. Local folk knew of tales attached to Bodkin Lane; the place was spoken of in hushed whispers, especially by the old ones. Gypsies and their caravans had long avoided the place; animals were fearful of it—that was always a good indicator that something was amiss. Gilly often heard young girls on horseback from a local riding school; their horses reared and snorted protestingly until the riders decided to take another route. Gilly would dance about in rage, cursing them for a mizzuble little herd, shouting his desire for a sugar stick to the surrounding countryside.

One spring day an enthusiastic teacher led a party of uniformed schoolgirls along the lane on a nature ramble. They were forced to abandon the project after thirteen-year-old Priscilla Long screamed and fainted at the sight of a ragged boy who materialized out of thin air. Pale and anxious Gilly had pranced around her shouting, "Where be your coach? Ha, Missie, ain't you or one o' your great herd got a sugar stick for Gilly, all dressed up in your strange finery like maypoles. Come on, out wi' your sugar sticks an' sweetmeats afore I goes mad!"

Priscilla had been nervously reaching for a packet of peppermints which she carried in her pocket when all nerve and senses deserted her. She shrieked and swooned away on the gravel path. One or two of the other girls were certain they had heard something and seen a dim shape. Their teacher took no chances; she swept Priscilla's limp form up and began hurriedly shepherding her charges back to school.

"Girls! Girls! Stop acting silly this instant! Form up into your groups. Jane, Mary, help me with Priscilla. Right, about turn and walk quietly back to the coach. Hurry up at the back there!"

Gilly followed them as far as he could, bellowing and shaking his fist. "Garn, I knew 'ee had a coach somewhere, fine ladies don't go afoot in these parts. Aye, an' I'll wager your coach is full of sweetmeats an' sugar sticks an' all. Mizzuble great herd, 'nuff to give a pore boy a worse 'eadache!"

When they had gone he went back to his boulder and ruminated darkly. "Huh, swoonin' an' screamin' females. I b'aint never goin' to get me a sugar stick at this rate."

But this time his pleas did not go unheeded. That day fate took a hand on Gilly Bodkin's side and wrought a small miracle.

Wayne Manfield Lee with his wife Tammy and their

four daughters came driving along Bodkin Lane. Tammy Manfield Lee was studying an ordnance survey map which she had spread across the dashboard of their "cute little English rental automobile, with a stickshift too." On the backseat their four overweight teenage daughers stuffed themselves with English candies from the airport shop. Wayne kept his eyes on the narrow gravelled path as he drove slowly along, debating with his wife.

"Honey, I'm not too sure they allow cars along this road. Are you sure this is the place?"

"I surely am. Look here, it says on the map: 'Site of Manfield Hall, seventeenth-century country manor.' We must be nearly there. Did your folks actually live here once?"

"Sweetie, they not only lived here, they owned the whole shebang, musta bin a couple hundred acres. Granmaw Manfield sure was right, my ancestors never hailed from the Panhandle in Texas; this was all Manfield country three hundred years back, lock, stock 'n' barrel."

One of the Manfield brood piped up from the rear seat.

"Is that why we're called Manfield Lee, Pop?"

Wayne shifted down to second gear as the car crunched along the gravel.

"Sure is, Connie. Granmaw looked up the records and it said that although Agnes Manfield came from England and married Hubert Lee, it was her one desire that the name Manfield be included in the family title. I guess that's why we're still called Manfield Lee. Hey, you guys in back there, don't make yourselves sick and poorly with all that English candy, y'hear."

Wayne's youngest daughter Agnes (named after her

illustrious ancestor) poked something sticky over the front seat.

"This candy's called barley sugar. It sure is neat. Have some, Daddy."

Wayne shook his head.

"Nope, kitten, I'll pass on that one. Candies are out with my cholesterol level. Say, see that old rock over there, I'll bet there's something carved on it like, 'One mile to Manfield Hall.' C'mon, let's stop and take a look."

Gilly had seen these horseless carriages before, but this was the first that had ever driven up his path since it had been gravelled by the workmen. The car halted. Gently rubbing his headache Gilly got off the boulder and went to investigate the curious conveyance.

The Manfield Lee family emerged. They stretched their legs and wandered over to the big boulder. Tammy was not very impressed.

"Hmm, it don't say nothing, Wayne. It's just an old rock, I guess."

"Right, honey, but it's a nice old rock, sorta homey looking. Say, look at all these old fields. I bet the Manfields used to grow squash and pumpkins and kale here."

The Manfield Lee girls were beginning to get bored.

"Oh, Poppa, come on. Let's go back to the hotel and watch English TV. Who wants to walk around some old field all day."

But Wayne led them further afield.

"Hey now, ladies, you're walking on history here. Wait'll I tell the folks back home about this. You got the camera, honey?"

"It's in the trunk. Hand me the keys, Poppa, I'll go get it."

Agnes walked back to the car. She was opening the trunk when she became aware she was not alone. A strange ragged barefoot boy was peering over her shoulder.

"You got any sweetmeats in there, Missie? Gilly wants a sugar stick."

Agnes was not surprised by anything in this strange country.

"Hi, I'm Agnes. Gilly? What sorta name's that, and what's a sugar stick? Don't they have sugar cubes or sachets over here?"

Gilly became quite excited.

"Sugar stick's a sweetmeat, Miss Agnes. Mercy me, I never thought you'd come back thisaways again. I never did."

"Silly, I've never been here before. Say, this sweetmeat or sugar stick or whatever you call it, is it some kinda candy? We've got a whole heap of English candies with us. You should try one. The barley sugar sticks are really neat. Would you like one, Gilly?"

Gilly Bodkin could not find the words to say. He stood on the gravel path, nodding dumbly, with great tears welling on to his cheeks. Agnes took a barley sugar stick from the car; she unwrapped it and offered it to her new-found friend.

"Gee, it's only an old barley sugar stick, Gilly. Don't get so upset; you can have lots of them if you like. We can always pick up more back at the hotel shop."

Gilly stretched out his hand. Amazingly he found he could touch the barley sugar stick. The first object he had been able to really feel in three hundred years, now he actually held it in his grimy hand. Gilly's eyes shone as he spoke in an awkward stammer.

"Thankee kindly, Missie Agnes, though I be afeared

now. I ain't never tasted no sugar stick. Be it sweeter'n apples? I tasted one of them once, long time ago."

Agnes laughed and clapped her hands.

"You bet it's sweeter than an apple. Go for it, Gilly, eat it."

Gilly took a bite. With an apprehensive look on his face he crunched and sucked at the sweetmeat it had taken him three hundred years to have. Agnes watched him, giggling with merriment at his grimaces. Gilly screwed up his face, squinted his eyes, pursed his lips and sucked his cheeks inward. Then he spat the barley sugar out on the gravel.

"Guuurrhhhgg! 'Tis far sweeter'n apples be, lack a day, mercy me! It be far too 'orrible sweet, 'tis enough to drive a poor lad to madness, all that sweetling. Harrgh! 'tis an 'ateful thing. My father were right, sweet things is only for gentryfolk an' beasts."

Dumbfounded, Agnes watched him begin to grow transparent before her eyes, his voice growing fainter as he spoke.

"Though I do be sorry I wasted 'ee sweetmeat, Missie Agnes. Lor' would you believe it, my 'eadache is ceased. O I do feel at peace now. Bless you, Missie, Gilly never thought to see you pass this way again. Thankee kindly and good fortune to you, Missie. . . ."

Agnes Manfield Lee watched in fascination as the wraithlike shape of Gilly Bodkin moved slowly to the boulder at the side of the path and disappeared completely, never to return. She dashed off to tell her family all about the strange event she had witnessed.

Wayne Manfield Lee sat his daughter upon the boulder and took several photographs (none of which later turned out). As the car drove off up the lane he studied

111

his daughter in the rearview mirror. She was sitting on the backseat with her sisters, eating English candies and discussing the ghostly occurrence. Wayne winked at his wife, and she smiled back understandingly. Young girls were forever imagining things; there was too much creepy stuff on television. Anyhow, in a few short years Agnes would discover boys in earnest and forget all this nonsense. Tammy passed a tissue box over to her daughters to wipe their sticky hands.

"Agnes honey, that surely is something, your first English ghost on your first visit over here. Wait'll we get home and tell Aunt Gail, though I wouldn't say too much to the kids at school. They'll think you're nutty. Keep it a secret to yourself, kitten."

The car purred off the gravel onto smooth tarmac, leaving the deserted path lying peacefully in its wake.

7

Bullies are a cowardly breed,
Vicious, nasty, yes indeed.
But this of course you probably know,
Having encountered a bully or so.
Bullies never smile, they sneer.
Bullies never laugh, they jeer.
And bullies never, as a rule,
Pick on someone big at school.
The innocent, the small, the weak,
Are easy targets that they seek.
The frightened and the not so sure,
Become the victims who endure
A twisted arm, a hard-tugged ear,
Torment, torture, shock and fear.
Bus fare, money meant for lunch,
Donated to some bullying bunch,
From little ones who sob through break,
Terrified! For goodness sake.
Wouldn't you just love to be
The one who stands courageously;
The one who has the guts to say,
"Bullies, you have had your day!"
Read on, dear reader young, read on,
You'll find there's hope for everyone.

R.S.B. Limited

There were three of them lounging at the school gates, two boys and a girl. They looked like trouble, all big and tough. Jonathan walked more and more slowly toward them, wishing he could suddenly turn and run away. Anywhere, as long as it was not in the direction of his new school and its bullies. His new school uniform made him stand out like a glacé cherry on a white frosted sandwich cake.

For the next two years Jonathan would be living in the house that had once belonged to his grandparents —Uncle Fred and Aunt Helen owned it now. He had been sent there by his father from the army camp. Jonathan had been brought up in army camps; his father was a soldier and was allowed to have his wife and child with him while on home posting. But now the regiment was going abroad, out east to what his dad described as a "political hotbed." Children weren't allowed out there. He complained long and loud that his mother would be going, but Dad was adamant. Jonathan had to go and live with his uncle and aunt. He recalled his father's parting words:

"Buck up, son, two years isn't a lifetime. You'll like Aunt Helen and Uncle Fred. Besides, this'll give you a chance at some proper education. Saint Michael's was your great-grandfather's old school, y'know. You'll see his name on the list in the assembly hall. Head prefect 1902 to 1903 Jonathan Coleman, same name as yourself."

Jonathan felt his cheeks flush bright red as he faced the trio of senior pupils blocking the school gates. The girl was very tall, taller than the two boys, one of whom was quite tall, while the other appeared quite runty.

114

She looked down her nose at Jonathan as if he were something she had trodden in. Taking a cigarette from her top pocket she turned to the smaller of the two boys; he lit it from a book of matches. A jet of smoke was directed into Jonathan's eyes and he blinked as the girl addressed him.

"Name?"

"Er, Jonathan."

"Jonathan what?"

"Jonathan Coleman."

The girl looked faintly amused; the two boys guffawed. Out of the corner of his eye Jonathan watched other pupils going into school by a gate further down. He decided to use that one in future. The girl spoke to him in a superior manner.

"So, a little coalman, eh? Well, we don't really need a coalman. Saint Michael's is centrally heated by gas now. See us at break, behind the sports equipment hut on the big field. Okay?"

Jonathan nodded dumbly.

The bigger of the two boys knocked the schoolbag from Jonathan's shoulder so that the contents spilled out on to the path. He picked up the can of cola and pocketed it, pointing a finger that touched the tip of Jonathan's nose. "See you at break, coalman, don't forget!"

They sauntered off laughing, leaving their victim behind to pick up his belongings and repack his bag.

Jonathan went through the routine formalities. This was not the first new school he had been in, though it was far older and larger than army camp schools. A vague, overweight principal told him how fortunate he was to be attending a school like Saint Michael's; a

115

twittering assistant principal said she hoped he would do as well as his great-grandfather, whose name was printed in gold on the assembly hall list. An indifferent school secretary took his particulars, illnesses, address, and names of relatives to contact. Jonathan missed breaktime—he was installed in a tiny room and given an aptitude assessment test paper by a Mrs. Van Horn, who said it was to determine his IQ. The boys and girls who were his classmates were pretty much the same as schoolchildren anywhere. They all knew each other, having gone through Saint Michael's together, and were not prepared to accept the new boy into their company right away. Jonathan was alone, a stranger, and acutely aware of it.

The buzzer sounded for lunch. Miserably Jonathan sat alone at a corner table in the canteen, eating ham sandwiches that tasted like blotting paper between ceiling tiles with soggy edges. He was drinking a glass of milk that he had bought at the counter when his empty cola can, crushed almost beyond recognition, slammed down on the tabletop. It was the tall boy. He touched the tip of Jonathan's nose with his finger again.

"Coalman, you didn't wash your ears out properly, or maybe you don't have much of a memory. You missed your appointment at break. Why?"

Jonathan stammered through a mouthful of ham sandwich and milk, "I was, er, had to test, er, assessment."

The tall boy smashed his fist down on the remaining sandwich. "Behind the sports hut. Now!"

He spun on his heel and swaggered off, helping himself to anything that caught his fancy as he passed between the tables. Nobody said a word or made a move to stop him.

116

The milk tasted sour in Jonathan's mouth as he turned out of the cafeteria into the main corridor. Standing at the far end was a boy his own age, and he looked very friendly. Jonathan smiled—he wanted to get to know the boy—but with a cheerful wave the boy skipped off down an intersecting corridor. Jonathan ran to catch up with him, but he reached the intersection in time to see the door to the sports field swing shut. Dashing down the passage he swung the door open.

"Aaaaahhhh!"

The tall boy had him by the ear. He twisted it savagely.

"Where did you get to, coalman? You're going to be late again. Miss Bingham doesn't like coalmen calling late, neither does Mr. Robbins, and as for Mr. Smith, well you can tell how I feel about it!"

Tugging at Jonathan's ear he marched him across the field. Through the tears forming in his eyes Jonathan could see no sign of the friendly boy he had encountered in the corridor.

Behind the sports equipment shed a girl of his own age was singing in a quavering voice:

"I saw three ships come sailing in,
On Christmas day in the morning."

The tall girl and her sly-looking accomplice were sitting on upturned garbage cans, watching the younger girl intently. Smith pushed Jonathan up against the side of the hut.

"Stand to attention there. We'll deal with you in a minute."

Smith took his place on an upturned garbage can.

117

The girl had finished singing, and the tall girl looked at her enquiringly.

"Well, what have you got to say for yourself, caroler?"

She answered meekly, "Please may I go, Miss Bingham?"

Robbins, the sly-looking one, shook his head.

"So you're still not paying up?"

The girl stood silent. Her three tormentors looked at one another, and Robbins shrugged philosophically.

"Righto, caroler, it's up to you, back here same time tomorrow. You can sing me 'Good King Wenceslas.' That's my favorite."

They dismissed the girl, but she stood watching as they turned their attentions to Jonathan. Bingham, the tall girl, lit a cigarette.

"Now, coalman, I'm Miss Charlotte Bingham."

She dabbed the cigarette in the direction of the runty boy. "This is Mr. Geoffrey Robbins, oh yes, and the gentleman who persuaded you to come here is none other than Mr. Malcolm Smith. We are the old school insurance firm, R.S.B. Limited. It's very simple, really, fifty pence a day and you're insured from annoyance and harassment by any pupil at Saint Michael's."

Smith grinned wickedly. "Especially us!"

Jonathan looked from one to the other.

"But I don't have any money."

"What about lunch money?"

"I bring sandwiches and a drink."

"Then what about bus fare?"

"I don't live far. I walk here."

"Hmm, you're in trouble, coalman, aren't you?"

"Er, yes."

"Yes, Miss Bingham."

118

"Er, yes, Miss Bingham."

"That's better! Right, Mr. Smith and Mr. Robbins, what do you think we should do with this horrible little creature until he decides to pay his insurance?"

Robbins dug away the grass with his heel until soil showed through. "He's a coalman, isn't he? We can't have him going about all nice and clean. As I remember, coalmen always have dirty faces, don't they?"

When he had been released Jonathan walked across the field with the girl who had been singing. She introduced herself. "My name's Kate Carroll—now you know why I've got to sing carols. Robbo, Smudger, and Bingo make me sing every day. Shall I help you to wash the mud off your face?"

Jonathan wiped a sleeve against his grimy cheeks.

"It's all right, I can do it, thanks. Are they always like that, Robbo, Smudger and Bingo?"

"Always. You'd better not let them hear you calling them Robbo, Smudger and Bingo. Everyone does, of course, but only behind their backs. Trouble is, there's nobody to stand up against them."

"Why doesn't someone report them to the principal?"

"That wouldn't do any good; no one'd back them up. Robbo was actually expelled last term for bullying, but the authorities made the school take him back. They said it was an isolated incident, high spirits and schoolboy horseplay. All Robbo had to do was apologize to the principal, not even to the boy whose books he tore up. They took him back like a shot. Saint Michael's can't afford to have their good name muddied by having pupils expelled because they can't control them."

119

"How long have you been singing for them, Kate?"

"Oh about two weeks or so. They won't bother with me after another week or two. I'm a difficult case, you see, I resist paying them. If they find that you're scared and pay up easy then it's worse— Robbo, Smudger and Bingo keep after you hard, and the payments go up. Be like me, Jonathan, stick it out until they get fed up with you."

"Without money I haven't got much choice, have I?"

"I don't have money either, that's why I face up to them. Look, I've got to go now, there's the buzzer. See you!"

"Bye, Kate, see you!"

Jonathan washed the streaks of mud from his face. He looked in the washroom mirror to check if he had missed any, and behind him he saw the boy who had been in the corridor earlier. He was smiling a warm, friendly smile. Jonathan turned around.

"Hello, my name's Jonathan, what's yours?"

The boy had gone. Jonathan swung the washroom door open. He looked up and down the corridor, but there was no sign of the strange boy. Going back to class Jonathan felt somehow easier and lighter. He felt that he could become friends with the boy, if only he could talk to him for long enough.

Robbo, Smudger and Bingo were waiting at the gate when school finished that afternoon. As Jonathan made his way to the gate lower down he heard Smith calling out to him.

"Over here, coalman. This is your gate, come on."

Reluctantly he faced the bullies. Bingo played with his tie as she spoke to him, tightening it bit by bit.

"Now don't forget to ask your mummy and daddy for lunch money. Say to them nicely, 'Please, mummy and daddy coalman, I want money.'"

"I can't, I live with my aunt and uncle. Aunt Helen says school meals are too expensive; she makes me take sandwiches."

"Well, does your uncle or aunt smoke? Cigarettes would do just as well as money."

"They don't smoke, either of them."

"You dirty little coalman, you're bound to get your face all mucky again, aren't you?"

"I s'pose so."

"You suppose so, Miss Bingham!"

"I suppose so, Miss Bingham."

An ancient car drove up with several older teenagers inside. The driver sounded his horn. Bingham gave the tie a final tug. "There's our ride, coalman. Don't forget and wash your face properly before you come to school tomorrow."

Jonathan loosened off his tie as he watched them roar off up the road.

Crossing the park he spotted the strange boy again, standing on the bridge over the boating lake. The boy smiled and waved to him, then he ducked out of sight below the parapet of the bridge. Jonathan knew it was a game the boy was playing. He decided to take part so that they could meet properly. Weaving in and out of the bushes like a soldier in jungle warfare he approached the bridge and dashed up the steps.

The boy was not there.

Jonathan looked over the bridge—there was nothing but water beneath. But there was the boy on the bandstand, conducting the empty seats on the rostrum as if a band were playing there. Waving his arms about, one hand open, the other clutching an imaginary baton, he leaned forward intently, just like a real band conductor. He turned with a mischievous grin and winked at Jonathan. Leaping down the bridge steps and keeping low in the bushes Jonathan sped toward the bandstand—knowing that his elusive friend would not be there, but enjoying the game.

He was correct. The boy had vanished again.

Jonathan scuffed the gravel with his shoes as he left the park. He was not too bothered. The boy had been wearing a Saint Michael's uniform, so sooner or later they would meet up in school. He wondered if the boy had ever been persecuted by Robbo, Smudger and Bingo. Probably not. There was something about him, despite his cheery, open appearance; something that hinted he was not to be messed about or pushed, a certain quality about the dark eyes and firm-set jaw. If they made friends and got to know one another, maybe the boy would help Jonathan. There he was again, peering from behind a tree on Chestnut Avenue. This time Jonathan did not give chase, he hid behind another tree and peered back. The two boys dodged along the length of the avenue, diving back and forth between the trees, waving, smiling at each other, and sometimes pulling grotesque funny faces. Jonathan approached the final tree stealthily, pretty sure that this time he would surprise his will-o'-the-wisp chum. The back flap of the boy's blazer was visible, poking around a tree trunk like a tiny red banner.

Jonathan sneaked up; grinning broadly he grabbed it tight. "Gotcha!" A red plastic supermarket bag hung limply from his hand.

Jonathan tossed it in the air, laughing aloud.

122

Whoever he was, that boy was certainly a fast mover. Laughter from the other side of the road mingled with his own. The strange boy was sitting on Jonathan's garden gate, swinging to and fro. Jonathan shook a fist and pulled a face of comic rage.

"I'll get you!"

The boy swung out of sight behind the gate column.

Jonathan searched the garden, behind the holly bush, around the lavender. He peered up into the beech tree. Nothing.

Climbing the side garden wall he thought he saw the boy, dodging off, hiding in gateways, peeking from bushes. As he disappeared along the avenue Jonathan waved to his friend.

"Jonathan! Get off that wall this instant!"

"Coming, Aunt Helen."

"I don't suppose your father would be too pleased if he saw you clambering up walls in your new school uniform. Don't have me writing to tell him. Come in for tea now."

Next day the insurance firm R.S.B. Limited stepped up its activities. Jonathan had to attend behind the sports hut at morning break, lunchtime and afternoon break. When he arrived there that afternoon Kate was singing in a mournful little voice:

"To save us all from Satan's power
When we have gone astray,
O tidings of comfort and joy, comfort and joy,
O tidings of comfort and joy."

Bingo flicked her cigarette away.

"Very good, caroler, I prefer that one to 'Good King

Wenceslas.' You can do it again in the morning."

Robbins interrupted.

"Unless you'd rather pay, let me see. Two school weeks and two days, that's six pounds."

Kate's face was straight, her voice expressionless. "I'd rather sing."

Smith dismissed her with a nod. "Coalman, you're next."

Kate stepped to one side as Jonathan stood in front of the trio. Smith accentuated each word by tapping Jonathan's nose.

"Bet you haven't brought any money with you today, eh?"

Jonathan shook his head dumbly. Robbins scuffed up dirt with his shoe. "Come on then, mucky face time again."

Wordlessly Jonathan placed his palms in the loose damp soil and began dabbing it on his cheeks. He made a point of not looking at anyone while he was doing it, telling himself in his mind that this was not happening to him, but to someone else. He looked over Kate's shoulder at the corner of the hut. The boy was there, poking his head around the corner, unseen by the others. He was smearing mud on his own face, shaking with silent laughter as if it were all some huge joke. Jonathan could not help it—he started laughing too, pantomiming his friend, smearing the mud in exactly the same way.

Robbins looked uneasy. "What's up with him, has he flipped his lid?"

The boy stuck out his tongue, waggling it. Jonathan roared with glee and imitated him. Bingo stood up, shaking her head.

"Come on, there's the buzzer. Let's get away from this nutcase."

124

When they had gone, Kate shook him by the sleeve.

"Jonathan, what on earth's the matter with you?"

Tears of laughter ran down his cheeks. He held his side with one hand as he pointed with the other.

"Oh hahaha! It's my friend, can't you see him, Kate!"

Kate gazed at the corner of the hut. "Where? I can't see anyone."

The boy had vanished again.

When Jonathan had his laughter under control, he tried explaining. Kate shook her head in disbelief as they walked back across the field. Nothing he said could convince her. She was becoming angry.

"All right then, describe him. What did he look like?"

"Oh, about my height, I suppose, dark brown hair, brown eyes, school uniform—looked a bit like me, I suppose."

Kate snorted. "Fibber! I've never seen anyone in school like that, 'cept you. You're just trying to make me look as big a fool as you."

"Kate, no, honestly, he was there—"

"I've got to go, I'm late for class already. You'd better clean that stuff off your face and get to class, too."

Jonathan watched her go, then something made him look upward. There was the boy again, still with mud on his face, looking out of the principal's office on the upper floor. He pressed his face flat against the window and blew out his cheeks. Jonathan roared anew with merriment and waved to him. "Be careful you're not caught."

The boy pulled in his chin, pointing to himself as if to say, "Me, get caught, don't be silly!"

Jonathan ran into the washroom laughing heartily.

125

Next morning Jonathan had a slight temperature. Nothing to worry about, Aunt Helen said, but he would be better staying in bed that day. He slept through the morning and by lunchtime was feeling much better. Aunt Helen allowed him to come downstairs and they lunched together in the kitchenette. She decided that he still looked a bit pale and should stay away from school until next day.

Jonathan messed about in the garden that afternoon; it was a fine sunny day. Finally he grew restless. There had been no sign of his friend all afternoon, though he had expected him to show up at any moment. Perhaps he could have cut classes and sneaked over to see him. He seemed the type who would do that for a friend. Maybe he would still come. Jonathan hoped he would.

Jonathan swung to and fro upon the gate, looking up and down the avenue; he even scrambled into the low branches of the beech tree to keep watch. But the strange boy never came that afternoon.

Kate had seen Jonathan several times at school that day, but she had not spoken to him for trying to take her for a fool the previous afternoon. He smiled as they passed on the corridor, looking as if he might try to stop and talk to her, but Kate held herself aloof, sweeping grandly past with her nose in the air. Jonathan did not turn up for his sessions with Robbo, Smudger and Bingo. They never said anything, though it was plain to Kate that they were working themselves up into a nasty mood. This meant trouble for them both. Silently disliking Jonathan for his silly behavior, she carried bravely on with her singing at the afternoon inquisition.

"To save us all from Satan's power
When we have gone astray. . . ."

126

"Go on, beat it, caroler. Get back to your class."

Bingo dismissed Kate and sat drumming her heels against the upturned garbage can. She was in a foul humor. Robbins and Smith waited instructions.

"Listen, you two, I want to see our little coalman, right after the last buzzer this afternoon. Don't let him sneak off, I'm going to teach him a lesson in manners he won't forget. Fancy missing three full sessions, the nerve of the cheeky beast!"

It was nearly 4.30 P.M. Every pupil had left the school, all of the staff too. Kate watched from behind the park gates where she could not be seen. Robbo, Smudger and Bingo had both exits from the school covered: Robbo and Smudger at the small gate, Bingo at the main one. Finally Jonathan came sauntering out.

Kate held her breath, trying desperately to control the butterflies that fluttered about inside her. Jonathan halted at the main gate, right in front of Bingo. He began talking coolly. Kate did not hear what went on, it was all a bit of an anticlimax. Bingo drew herself to her full height, eyes narrowed, jaw set. She stared down her nose at Jonathan, who did not seem at all impressed. He exchanged some brief words with her, passed her something, then went on his way.

Kate breathed a sigh of relief; at least he was safe and unharmed. Come to think of it he had acted rather boldly; there had been no trace of the humble coalman about him. Jonathan caught sight of her and waved cheerily, then he dodged behind a tree. In spite of her former mood Kate smiled and waved back. She dashed to the tree, but he was gone. He popped from behind another tree, then another, leading her along. Kate ran

127

after him calling, "Stop, Jonathan, stop. Come out, I know you're there!"

But he was not. Jonathan was behind the park gatepost, then he was hiding in the bushes, next he was waving from the bridge. Kate began to lose her happy mood; the chase was irritating her. "Jonathan, stop right there. I have to talk to you!"

Gone again? She could stand it no longer. Standing on the bridge she watched him on the bandstand conducting an imaginary band. Why wouldn't he speak to her? Why didn't he stop in one place until she caught up with him? Look at him, waggling his arms about with that idiotic grin on his face. Her hands gripped the stone lintel of the bridge tightly as she shouted aloud, "You're stupid, Jonathan Coleman, stupid and silly, d'you hear me? I never want to speak to you again. Think you're clever, don't you! Go on, laugh, but Robbo, Smudger and Bingo will have the last laugh, and you needn't come crying to me. So there!"

She flounced angrily off across the park, her cheeks bright red.

Smith and Robbins leaned over Bingham's shoulder as she read the note Jonathan had passed to her.

> "I'll give you ten pounds for the coalman and another ten for the caroler if you promise to leave us alone. Be at the back of the hut on the sports field tomorrow night at eleven.
>
> Jonathan Coleman"

Robbins whistled through his teeth. "What d'you make of that?"

Smith sniggered. Bingham silenced him with a glare.

"It means that our coalman has got money from somewhere, quite a bit of it too. He's trying to buy insurance for himself and the little caroler. Do you know what that means?"

"He's in love!"

Bingham looked down her nose at Robbins.

"It means that if he can get his hands on that much money, there's bound to be more. He can pay up again and again, if we play this right."

"Suppose it's some kind of trap?"

Bingham folded the note pensively.

"No, I don't think so. He's too innocent for something like that. But you could be right, I suppose. We'd better take out some insurance to cover ourselves in that case. Tomorrow night, you two get up on top of the sports hut, that way you'll get a good view all around. If any parents, teachers or police are with him, we can beat it, long before they ever get to the hut. Guess who'll look foolish then, telling stories to get others in trouble and wasting other people's time at dead of night on a wild goose chase."

Robbins began giggling again; so did Smith. She joined them.

It was a perfect plan.

Next morning Jonathan walked through the school gates unhindered—the three bullies were not waiting there. Kate swept regally past him, ignoring his cheerful hello. As he went into school something made him glance backwards. His strange friend was standing on the roof of the sports hut, laughing and holding both thumbs up. Jonathan smiled and gave a thumbs-up in return before going into assembly.

At break time he went to the session behind the hut.

Kate was there but their tormentors were not. Jonathan looked around.

"Where is everybody today?"

Kate bit her quivering lip. "Prob'ly hiding like you were yesterday."

"Hiding? I wasn't hiding anywhere. I was sick!"

She stamped her foot angrily. "You're sick, all right! Jonathan the vanishing boy, Jonathan the grinning idiot, why don't you run off and hide somewhere now? I'm going in, there's the buzzer."

Kate stormed off, leaving Jonathan sad and perplexed.

At lunchtime he stayed alone in the canteen; nobody bothered him. Kate avoided the canteen and went out onto the field for lunch. As she passed the hut Bingham darted out and caught her by the back of her neck.

"Come on, caroler, behind here. The old firm wants a word with you!"

Robbins and Smith were there, perched on the upturned garbage cans. Kate looked hopefully at them.

"I came this morning but you weren't here. Do you want me to sing?"

Bingham thrust the note under Kate's nose. "What's this all about?"

Kate read it, her eyes wide with disbelief. "I don't know, honest."

Smith drummed his heels against the garbage can. "Oho, I'll bet you don't."

Bingham's eyes were dangerously cruel. She pulled Kate's ponytail, waggling her head back and forth.

"Listen, you. That money better get here on the dot tonight. Tell your friend that if he tries any fancy tricks we'll make an example of you both that this school will never forget. Now beat it quick!"

Kate ran off with hot tears welling in her eyes, wishing that she had never met Jonathan. Running off, grinning, hiding, playing tricks then acting the innocent, and now this. She saw him watching her from the science room window; he was smiling and nodding to her. Tight lipped, Kate stopped to gather a handful of gravel from the path. Before she could raise her arm to throw it at the window he was gone. It was all too much. She broke down and cried, rubbing her eyes with dusty hands until her face became grubby and tearstained.

A chilly night breeze had sprung up, it chased a page of yesterday's newspaper across the dry turf of the sports field. Robbins strained his eyes against the darkness.

"Something's moving out there. Maybe it's him!"

Bingham pulled out a cigarette, watching the deserted field carefully.

"It's only a piece of paper. Stop yelling all over the place, will you! Anyone got a light?"

Smith produced matches. He tried lighting the cigarette for her but the wind blew the match out. He giggled nervously. Bingham gave him a cold stare. "Will you two stop acting like a pair of little kids, sniggering and getting excited over bits of paper."

Robbins slumped moodily against the hut.

"We're only keeping a lookout. It's pitch black out there, you know."

Bingham took the matches and lit the cigarette herself.

"Well of course it is, genius. It is nighttime, after all. Wait a sec, what was that?"

"What was what?"

Bingham's voice dropped to a whisper. "Over there in the doorway."

Robbins laughed scornfully.

"Now who's acting like a little kid, eh! It's only some newspaper; the wind's blown it into the passage doorway. Look!"

He ran off toward the school building, glad to have something to do other than stand about. Diving into the darkened doorway recess he caught the windblown paper and waved it aloft.

"See, I told you, yesterday's *Daily Mail*." He let it flutter from his grasp to be carried away on the breeze. "Whooo! Look, a ghost!"

Smith watched the paper lifting above the school building. He gave a small whimper and went rigid. Robbins arrived back panting.

"Whew! It's hard running after ghosts. What's up with him?"

Bingham turned to Smith. He stood ashen and shaking, his finger pointing. "Th . . . th . . . there, first-floor staff-room window. He was there!"

She grabbed him by his blazer collar. "Who was?"

"Him! The coalman. He was watching us, laughing."

Bingham threw the cigarette down and ground it savagely with her heel.

"Right, that's it! Frightened to death by a piece of paper blowing past a windowpane. It was only a reflection, you dimwit. And you, Robbins, you're as bad, prancing about like a two-year-old. 'Whooo! Look, a ghost!' Listen, if we want to make twenty pounds tonight and more in the future you two had better stop acting soft. Now get up on the roof of that hut and keep watch."

Cowed by the big girl's temper the pair climbed on the garbage cans and hauled themselves up to the flat roof of the hut. Smith was about to remind her that it was she who started the panic by sighting the newspaper in the doorway, when a heavy gust of wind caused him to drop on all fours. He complained unhappily.

"Hey, this wind's getting up to gale force. We could be blown off."

Bingham was in no mood for complaints.

"Shut up whining, Smith. Keep your eyes open and let me know the moment you see the kid coming, or anyone at all. We might have to hoppit quick if he's snitched to the teachers or the police."

The minutes ticked by and Bingham began to grow uneasy. Maybe the little rat would bring some adult help. But they were committed now, the prospect of twenty pounds for a bit of bullying was too good to pass up. Eight for her and six pounds apiece for the other two. She drew her collar up against the keening wind and waited. Robbins's voice interrupted her thoughts.

"Here he comes. He's just stepped out of the bushes on the far side."

"Good, is he alone?"

"Wait, let him get out on to the field a bit."

"If you see anyone with him get down off there right away, you two."

"No, it's okay. He's all on his own. Haha, come to us, little coalman."

"Cut the comedy and keep your eyes peeled. They could come in from either side to trap us."

"Ha, no chance. Apart from this wind there's only us and him. He's as cold as us; he looks very pale and chilled."

133

Now Bingham could see Jonathan clearly.

"No wonder, he's only got his school uniform on. But who's worried, as long as he's got the money with him."

Without warning the wind died away completely. Now the pale-faced boy stood in front of them. He was smiling, but it was not a pleasant smile. Behind Bingham the three garbage cans took off across the windless field with a nerve-jangling clatter. Then there was silence, total and complete, the gloom pressing in on the three bullies. Bingham knew without looking that the other two were utterly petrified. She tried to shrug off the feeling. Moistening her tongue and swallowing hard, she did her best to sound cool and arrogant. "Well, coalman, brought the money?"

The boy had stopped smiling. He raised a hand and the wind sprang up again with renewed fury. His appearance began changing before their astonished gaze.

He grew taller, much bigger and broader too. Lines and wrinkles creased inexplicably across his face; the eyes narrowed, burning with a terrifying intensity. No longer was he a boy in school uniform; now he was a fully grown man, tall and severe, dressed in a long-gone fashion. He wore a black frock-coated suit, and beneath his eight-buttoned waistcoat a stiff white shirt gleamed, surmounted by a black bow tie. The man's powerful hands played idly with a gold watch fob and chain strung across the front of his waistcoat, his face a mask of forbidding authority, broad nostrils quivering fitfully over a stiff, waxed mustache.

Smith and Robbins had fallen to their knees on the roof of the hut, the wild wind chilling their bloodless faces as it tore at open mouths. The man's dark hair was

134

neatly combed in an old-fashioned middle parting, not a hair of it moved in the howling gale as he nodded his head solemnly at the hut. It shook and trembled, and the two boys on top fell flat on their faces. Now the hut began to rise from the ground. Up, up it travelled, ascending into the empty starless skies of the storm-filled night, high above the darkened planet. Smith and Robbins grasped the edges of the roof, too terrified even to shut their eyes as they stared out into the dim reaches of the universe. The school grounds far below were not even a dot on the map as they hovered in empty space, yet like overhead thunder they heard the voice of the man as he spoke to the girl on the ground.

"I have brought the money. Take the rewards of your cowardice!"

Bingham had fallen upon her knees. The wind whipped through her hair and stung her eyes, yet she could not take them off the apparition that stood before her, unruffled by the howling gale. Slowly the man put finger and thumb into his vest pocket and drew forth four large outdated white five-pound notes. He held them out to her, his voice booming like a cathedral bell tolling requiem.

"Vile creature! Grovelling wretch! Take the price of the misery you have caused!"

His eyes bored into her very soul as with nerveless fingers she reached out and touched the money.

A crackling flash of forked lightning ripped the night sky apart. Thunder banged overhead like the crashing of the gates of doom.

The girl's screams were mingled with those of her two companions as the sports hut plunged earthward—they wailed like lost souls in the pits of fear. The hut hit the field, shattering into matchwood, throwing Smith and Robbins senseless in the dirt alongside Bingham. She knelt on the ground, clutching a torn piece of newspaper in one hand as she smeared dirt on her face with the other. The man had gone, but the smiling boy stood watching her for a moment before walking off into the calm windless night.

In Saint Michael's next morning Jonathan stood next to Kate. The assembly hall was packed to the doors with silent pupils. The staff sat on stage, flanking the principal, a police superintendent and a doctor from the local hospital. Immediately after the school anthem had been sung, the principal stood up on the rostrum. He addressed the pupils in his stern morning voice.

"Certain events took place on the sports field of this school last night which you may or may not be aware of. Let me dispel any foolish tales or rumors you may have heard by telling you precisely what happened. I hope this will also serve as a warning to any would-be trespassers or vandals. What I have to tell you will be amply borne out by Superintendent Atherton and Doctor Pradesh, who attended the three pupils involved. At about 11 P.M. last night there was a short-lived, but extremely powerful freak storm. Charlotte Bingham, Geoffrey Robbins and Malcolm Smith, three sixth-graders, were in the school grounds without permission. At some point these unfortunate trespassers were playing around the school sports hut when it was struck by lightning. Fortunately none of them was killed. When the police arrived on the scene they found the hut totally demolished. Smith and Robbins were both unconscious, and although Bingham had not been injured she was in a very distressed state. Doctor Pradesh tells me that it is unlikely they will ever be able to return to Saint Michael's again, though with proper psychiatric counselling and medical care they will return to normal life in due course.

"So let me repeat a warning that you have, no doubt, been given often by your teachers. You will not, I repeat, not, use this school as an adventure playground or meeting place when you have no business here. Once you leave school each afternoon, it's straight home, unless told otherwise by myself or your teachers. Three children who ignored school rules are now lying in hospital—imagine the concern they have caused, to their parents, police, hospital staff, their teachers and myself. Bingham, Robbins and Smith are regretting now that they ignored warnings and school rules; let us hope that you will learn from what happened to them in their disobedience, and stay clear of unattended school grounds after hours. Do I make myself clear?"

Jonathan and Kate joined in the mass chorus of "Yes, sir!" but they were not looking at the principal. They were both gazing out the window at the smiling boy who was waving goodbye to them from the wreckage of the sports hut.

DATE DUE

GAYLORD   #3523PI   Printed in USA